"It's some kind of [joke]," [said]
Joanne fearfully. It wa[s hard to believe]
that the entire basketball team, including her
husband, was being held for ransom.

"I'm afraid it's no joke, Joanne," replied
Hondo quietly.

"Please, Lieutenant," Joanne begged in an-
guish, "you have to get them out of there!
Give them what they want, but please, get
Ollie and the others out of there!"

"We'll do the best we can, Joanne, but we
can't make any deals."

And once again, a life-and-death decision
was all his to make, alone. . . .

———————————

Based upon the Television Series
"S.W.A.T."
Created by ROBERT HAMNER
Developed by RICK HUSKY
Adapted from the episode "Red September"
Story by LARRY ALEXANDER
Teleplay by ROBERT HAMNER
and LARRY ALEXANDER

CROSSFIRE!
is an original POCKET BOOK edition.

CROSSFIRE!

by

DENNIS LYNDS

Based upon the Television Series "S.W.A.T."
Created by ROBERT HAMNER
Developed by RICK HUSKY
Adapted from the episode "Red September"
Story by LARRY ALEXANDER
Teleplay by ROBERT HAMNER
and LARRY ALEXANDER

PUBLISHED BY POCKET BOOKS NEW YORK

CROSSFIRE!

POCKET BOOK edition published November, 1975

This original POCKET BOOK edition is printed from brand-new plates made from newly set, clear, easy-to-read type. POCKET BOOK editions are published by POCKET BOOKS, a division of Simon & Schuster, Inc., 630 Fifth Avenue, New York, N.Y. 10020. Trademarks registered in the United States and other countries.

1

The small black sedan drove slowly along the street of two-story apartment houses in the bright California sunlight. None of the strollers clad in shorts and bikini tops looked twice at the car as it pulled to the curb, or at the two men who got out.

One, the driver, was a slim man in his thirties, dressed in slacks, sport shirt, and dark blue blazer. He was hard looking, with quick movements and hidden muscles; he looked like an overage running back.

"You know what you have to do, Cortease?" he said.

The second man nodded. In his late twenties, small and stocky, he was intense and nervous. He carried an attaché case.

"I know my job, okay?" he said.

The driver watched the younger man, his eyes studying him, hard and cold. The younger man was annoyed.

"Don't worry about me, McVea," he snapped.

"But I do worry, Nick," McVea said. "A great deal is riding on this operation—a lot of people are depending on you. You're sure you can handle it?"

"I can handle it," Nick Cortease said. It came out quick and intense.

Too quick. The older man, McVea, rubbed at his lean jaw, considered his nervous companion.

"What is it, Nick? You worried about going back inside?"

Cortease looked up and down the sunny street. "They catch me, it's a long jolt in the slammer."

"Not if you play it right, the way we planned. Besides, what makes you think you'll get caught? You're a pro, and up on the roof you've got plenty of time for a getaway. The fuzz don't move fast and never could climb."

"Yeh, I guess you're right," Cortease said.

"A clean getaway, and if anything does go wrong it's one, maybe two years on ice. For a hundred Gs. Fifty big ones a year, pretty good pay for taking a vacation in Vacaville."

Cortease grinned now. "Yeh, I always did like that kind of arithmetic, McVea. Well, here we go."

He turned and started up the sunny street carrying the attaché case.

"Nick?" McVea said behind him. "Haven't you forgotten something?"

Cortease turned back, scowling. McVea leaned into the black car and came out with a stack of printed pamphlets.

"You go up and start shooting without these and we accomplish nothing, damn it!"

"I forgot 'em, okay?" Cortease said.

"Don't forget anything else!" McVea said, his voice harsh and stony. "The pamphlets first, then shoot up all hell. You understand that?"

"Okay, okay," Cortease said.

"No more mistakes, Nick, you got it?"

The smaller man nodded, took the stack of pamphlets. In violent reds and blacks, with crude drawings of men raising their guns high, the pamphlets proclaimed: "The Organization for the Freedom of Oppressed Peoples—Red September, the Hour of retribution is near!"

Nick Cortease walked away and turned into an apartment building. McVea watched him go, his dark eyes gleaming, a smile on his hard face.

Lieutenant Dan Harrelson, team leader of the Olympic S.W.A.T. unit, W.C.P.D., wasn't listening to the important local columnist in the team's E.C. room on the second floor of the precinct. The columnist didn't like that—he was used to people being impressed by him. Harrelson didn't seem impressed.

"Special Weapons and Tactics—S.W.A.T.," the columnist said. "A lot of people don't think such units are necessary, a waste of taxpayers' money. Some say S.W.A.T. isn't even desirable—at best an arrogant elite unit using too much force, at worst a gang of trigger-happy storm troopers."

Chief Howard Roman sounded uneasy as he gave his stock reply. "Federal authorities acknowledge S.W.A.T. units to be the most advanced and effective strike force against contemporary urban crime. If that wasn't true, I wouldn't have started the units in the W.C.P.D."

"That's a press release, Chief," the columnist said. "I'd rather hear what the lieutenant has to say—in his own words. He's the trained man, the expert, right? Are you training legal killers, Lieutenant?"

"What?" Harrelson said, obviously distracted.

"We're not training killers," Deacon Kay said quickly. "We're training policemen who can think fast, react fast, and handle tough situations dangerous to the whole city."

Second in command of the S.W.A.T. team, Kay was a huge black policeman who'd spent half his forty-odd years on the force.

"I've seen a lot of innocent people and a lot of good cops hurt because no one knew how to handle violence," Deacon Kay went on. "Without special weapons, and without training in handling riots, sniper

7

attacks, shoot-outs, big robberies, the police can't work efficiently. Then things get out of hand."

Chief Roman said, "Deke is Lieutenant Harrelson's assistant here. He's a regular S.W.A.T. man too, training this unit."

"I'd still like to hear from the lieutenant," the columnist said. "Maybe he doesn't want a feature story? Maybe he doesn't like explaining himself to concerned citizens?"

"Sorry," Harrelson said, making an effort to smile at the columnist. "I was thinking. Now, what was it you asked?"

"Hondo Harrelson," the columnist said. "That's your nickname, isn't it? Sounds tough, military, almost arrogant. Green Beret stuff, search and destroy. Do we need that here?"

In the silent E.C. room they all watched Harrelson —the chief, the other four members of the S.W.A.T. unit, and the columnist.

The lieutenant's voice was quiet and terse. "I was a Green Beret in Viet Nam, yes," he said evenly. "But I was a cop before that, mister, and I'm a cop now. No, we don't need Viet-Nam-style search-and-destroy units here, but we can learn from them. We can learn that inexperienced, untrained people can be a menace more than a help in a dangerous situation. I pinned on my badge when I was twenty-one, and by the time I was twenty-three I'd killed two men in the line of duty. At least one of them I might not have had to kill if I'd known what I know now."

James Street, the young, intense scout of the team, spoke up now. "I think most cops who've had to kill someone would say that, sir. Skill and training can prevent killings."

"It can," Harrelson agreed softly. "I put six years in on the first S.W.A.T. team down in L.A. applying what I'd learned in Viet Nam—and what I'd learned as a kid patrolman down there. When Chief Roman asked me to come and start units here, I did. Because I'd learned that the best way to fight violent urban crime today is with a small, disciplined unit using special weapons, tactics, and training designed to neutralize big firepower and unusual force situations. Quick, hard, and sure counterattack gives the lowest danger to innocent citizens—and to the police."

"Right on, Lieutenant!" Dominic Luca cried, his urchin, broken-nosed, dead-end-kid face all grin.

"You tell him, Hondo," T. J. McCabe echoed admiringly, his boyish face agreeing all the way.

Jim Street said, "Maybe we overreact sometimes —all cops do, because we're human. We make mistakes, but trained men make fewer of them. If we do our job, we end trouble faster, and hopefully without any violence. When we get really good, we'll probably *prevent* violence turning into a riot or worse."

Hondo Harrelson smiled. "Do they sound like robot killers or storm troopers? I think maybe my team can speak for us better than I can. Meet them, mister." He pointed: "That half-pint roughneck is Dominic Luca, our rearguard man. He eats too much pizza and he talks out of turn, but when I've got him behind me with his 12-gauge shotgun I don't worry about what might be at my rear."

He nodded at the blond T. J. McCabe. "McCabe is our sniper. Maybe he looks like the All-American boy, and he should be playing pro sport—you name the sport—but he's a good cop, and his dad was a good cop before him."

James Street spoke before Harrelson could turn to him. "I'm Street, the team scout. I used to ask those questions you did, mister, and sometimes I still do. Maybe because I still haven't made up my mind whether I'll be a cop or a lawyer. But I'm not sure the city doesn't need trained cops more than lawyers."

Hondo said, "Street'll drive an old cop crazy always asking 'Why?' But I guess old cops learn, too, when they have to try to say 'why' they do something." He looked at Deacon Kay. "The Chief told you about Deke there. He studied to be a priest once, he's been a cop a long time, he's got four kids—two of them are adopted, and he never can remember which two. He's my second, and my friend."

Harrelson nodded to the columnist. "That's Olympic S.W.A.T. They can tell you all you need to write your feature. Listen to them. Excuse the chief and me now—we've got work."

Harrelson turned and walked toward his private office. A tough-faced, masculine-looking man in his forties, he moved with powerful strides. The chief followed him into his office and closed the door. Roman studied his S.W.A.T. team leader as Harrelson sat down at his desk.

"He's important to me, Hondo," Roman said. "Important to us, to S.W.A.T. His Sunday column has a hell of a lot of readers in this city. We need public acceptance."

"Sorry," Harrelson said tersely. "We've got a job, too."

"Those messages?" the chief said. He sat down. "Any more of them reported?"

"No," Harrelson said. "Just the four—four telephone calls to the department in one week: 'The Organization for the Freedom of Oppressed Peoples will strike soon! Be prepared, lovers of Zionist pigs, for the Red September. Lock your doors, hide in your banks, but you can't stop us—first a scratch, a cut, and then the mortal blow!' Four of the calls, voices muffled. All warnings, Chief."

"Crackpots," Chief Roman said. "Or some cranks giving us a war of nerves. All talk, no action."

"Maybe," Harrelson said.

His cool, wind-creased eyes went distant. . . .

They were holed up in the tenement basement, blasting the street with volleys of gunfire. Two bitter old men who'd never had a home outside the Communist Party; three reform-school boys who'd found a new way of life—a Cause; two street girls kicked out of high school into the arms of the self-proclaimed revolutionary group; and one college girl who'd read too many political books. Eight. nobodies with two shotguns, three old hunting rifles, one .22, and a ten-dollar pistol. That had been it, the whole "Revolutionary Army." But the Captain hadn't known that then, and neither had a twenty-two-year-old fire-eating patrolman named Dan Harrelson. "Hell, Captain, we'll just walk in and grab 'em." The captain asked for instructions; he knew about muggings, burglaries, criminals, but this . . . ? The brass said, crackpots, they'll fold, you can't let them bluff us. Move fast, Captain, protect the public. "Punks, all talk," tough, young Dan Harrelson had said. "Let's go in and blast 'em out Captain." And when the blasting was over fifteen bodies lay in that street: six of the "revolutionaries," four policemen, four innocent citizens of the city, and Captain Walter Dawson. . . .

Hondo Harrelson blinked, looked down at the report of the four telephone calls.

"All talk," Chief Roman said. "Nothing's happened, Dan."

"Not yet," Lieutenant Hondo Harrelson said.

2

Douglas McVea stood in the doorway, shadowed from the sunny street, and looked across the street and upward. He watched the roof parapet of the apartment directly across until he saw a head appear. A furtive head, and a pair of quick eyes that looked and then vanished. McVea smiled. Cortease was in position.

McVea looked up and down the quiet street, but there was nothing to see except the ordinary cars of ordinary people. He looked back up at the parapet of the apartment building. There was movement up there, vague and unidentifiable, but McVea could imagine what was happening, could picture it in his mind. Cortease had opened the attaché case, taken out all the smooth, intricate metal parts. Excited, Cortease was fitting the pieces together into the slim, lethal automatic rifle.

McVea felt the excitement himself, an almost sensual pleasure. He could see Cortease's hands fumbling a little as he assembled the rifle, the way a man's hands fumble with the buttons of the dress of a woman he wants. There was something beautiful about a smooth, blue steel rifle, something beautiful and deadly like a woman. *More* beautiful than a woman, McVea thought—something you could count on, something a man could trust. A rifle in your hands, power . . . !

The limousine appeared at the head of the quiet street.

McVea shook himself from his reverie, licked his

12

lips once, glanced quickly up toward the parapet across the street. The quick wave of a hand, there and gone, told him that Cortease had seen the limousine —the ambassador's car.

McVea calculated swiftly—the ambassador would be within range of the parapet in one minute.

He left the shadowed doorway and walked up the street to a telephone booth out of sight of the roof parapet. He picked up the receiver, dropped in his dime, and dialed.

"Operator! Get me the police! An emergency!"

The great black limousine was moving slowly in the traffic, preceded and followed by a small police escort.

"Hello! Yes, you've got to get here fast. What? No, no, I'm calling from Fourteenth and Northern, there's no time! Some crazy bastard is shooting all hell out of the street! Yeh, from a roof! Hurry!"

McVea hung up, smiled wolfishly, and stepped from the phone booth. The limousine was almost directly in front of where Nick Cortease crouched up behind the parapet with his rifle. McVea hurried to his small sedan, opened the door, and paused for a second to look back at the ambassador's limousine and then up at the building where Cortease waited. He saw the slim barrel of the rifle slide out like the tongue of some deadly snake. McVea nodded and smiled again.

"Go, baby," he said softly to himself. "Fire when ready."

Then he got into his sedan and drove away fast.

In his private command office at Olympic S.W.A.T., Lieutenant Hondo Harrelson gripped the receiver tightly as he listened to the urgent voice at the other end.

"Ten-four, Communications," Hondo barked, "we're on the way now!"

13

He was up and out into the E.C. room in three long strides, his mind wiped clear of everything but the need for immediate action. Deacon Kay saw him first and jumped up when he saw the lieutenant's expression.

"What's up, Hondo?"

Street, Luca, and T. J. McCabe were on their feet, too. It looked like action.

"Man just called in," Hondo said, walking past them to the arsenal room. "A sniper's shooting up the city a couple of blocks from here—Fourteenth and Northern."

"Sniper?" T. J. said.

"Anyone hurt?" Street wanted to know.

"So what are we waiting for?" Dominic Luca said. "Let's roll!"

"Yeh," Hondo said, "let's roll—and fast!"

They all crowded into the arsenal, grabbed their weapons, blue flak jackets, walkie-talkies, beepers, and other S.W.A.T. equipment, and ran out of the E.C. to where their van waited.

In seconds the van was out in the street and heading for Fourteenth and Northern Boulevard, its top-light whirling red, its siren screaming through the sunny afternoon.

At Fourteenth and Northern people were screaming, screaming and running for cover in the bright sunlight.

The ambassador's limousine had been stopped by the first shot, which had blown out its left front tire, and was parked at an angle across the street. The police escort had slewed to a violent stop, the patrolmen spreading out.

Up on the parapet of the two-story building, Nicholas Cortease stood tall at the edge, his rifle held high and defiant above his head. His eyes shining, his legs spread wide in bold challenge, he hurled his pamphlets down toward the now almost empty street. The gaudy leaflets fluttered in the air, and the terrified, confused people in the street grabbed at them.

"Read them, yes!" Cortease shouted from the rooftop. "Read the truth and understand, you bloated Yankee dogs!"

The stocky man on the roof laughed maniacally. He lowered his automatic rifle from above his head, cradled it in the crook of his left arm, and sprayed a wild fusillade above the heads of the people below.

"Infidels!" he shouted. "Zionist pigs! Read the word of true revolutionists and know that your time has come!"

He sprayed another long volley into the brick of the buildings across the street.

"You will no longer oppress the innocent people of the world, grow fat on the suffering of the world! The time of retribution is at hand! You will no longer oppress the true believers, drive innocent people from their homelands! Listen and remember! This is a last warning!"

Another volley hammered from the automatic rifle, showering brick chips and dust down into the street, smashing glass, the bullets whining away. . . .

There was a scream from the street.

A woman, hit by a ricocheting bullet, fell bleeding and clutching at her shoulder.

On the roof Nicholas Cortease seemed to freeze as he looked down at the fallen woman and the two men bending over her. His manic eyes were glazed.

The ambassador, a small, dark man in a neat business suit, fought off the hands of the aides who tried to stop him and stepped out from behind the limousine where he'd taken cover. He was pale, his hands shook, but he looked straight up toward Nicholas Cortease, and his voice rang out clearly. "Young man!

This is no way to gain recognition! To make people listen to your cause, you must—"

Cortease blinked down at the ambassador, his eyes wild and violent.

"Fat pig!" he shouted, suddenly lowering his rifle and firing straight at the ambassador.

The ambassador dove to the concrete of the street, and hands unceremoniously dragged him behind the cover of the limousine. Unhurt, he stood up at once, brushing himself off.

"You fat son-of-a-bitch!" the sniper screamed.

The automatic rifle raked the limousine from end to end, shattering the windows, tearing and ripping the metal. Cortease swung the gun right and left, sweeping the open street, pumping bullets straight down now.

"All you smug sons-of-bitches!"

The people on the street ran over each other in panic as the bullets hit, ricocheting off the concrete and whining like angry insects through the street.

A police car exploded as its gas tank was hit. It burned fiercely on the sunny street.

A policeman was down, bleeding and crawling for safety.

A fat, middle-aged man in a grimy T-shirt puffed in terror for the cover of a culvert. He didn't make it, and he fell with his fat legs jerking in spasms, his blood spreading around him in a widening pool.

A cameraman, leaning on the hood of his radio car, aimed his telephoto lens up toward the roof as Cortease continued to fire. A bullet caught the cameraman between the eyes. He was dead before his body hit the street, his camera flying through the sunlight to smash on the sidewalk.

On the roof, Nicholas Cortease began to shout all the obscenities he had learned in his twenty-plus years

16

on the slum streets of the city. In his hoarse voice there was all the hate of those long, violent years.

Laughing, cursing, screaming down into the bloody street, he went on firing, changing clips, and firing again, and never noticed the blue van swinging into the street at the far end and coming to a stop.

3

The S.W.A.T. team spread out from the van, which was now blocking the end of the street. Dominic Luca and T. J. McCabe took the left side of the street and the cover of a low brick stoop and a row of garbage cans. Deacon Kay, Street, and Hondo sprinted low, zigzagging to the right side and an abandoned truck. From behind it they had a clear view of the sniper high on his rooftop. Hondo took in the whole situation with a quick sweep of the street ahead.

"Three down!" Jim Street said, his AR–15 aimed straight up at the rooftop.

"Four," Deke Kay said, and he pointed to where a policeman sat against a distant building holding his shoulder with one hand and his service pistol with the other. "One of our guys is hit."

"Looks like he missed the ambassador, though," Street said, nodding toward the limousine in the middle of the shattered street.

Hondo Harrelson wasn't listening to his men. His cool, wind-creased eyes were studying the situation and terrain. He could see at a glance that the sniper had picked his position well. The apartment building

17

was set back slightly from the sidewalk, giving the sniper a clear shot directly in front and all the way to both ends of the street. To the right of the building there was a narrow, open parking lot the sniper could cover. Hondo was pretty sure the rear door of the building would be locked inside, and breaking it in would alert the sniper. And the only building with a roof slightly higher than the one the sniper occupied was a good four hundred yards away on the next street.

"He's got all the front entrances zeroed in," Hondo said, his decisions made. "But I can see an open window on the ground floor. One of us ought to be able to get inside that way, work up to the roof—if we can get across that parking lot."

"No sweat, Lieutenant," Jim Street grinned. "He won't even see my smoke."

"Maybe the rest of us oughta go home," Deke said. "We've got us a one-man army."

"First," Hondo said, ignoring them, "there's a building over there a little higher. I want—"

The firing, exploding in the distance the whole time they'd been there, suddenly seemed louder.

"Down!" Deke cried.

Hondo, Street, and Deke hit the dirt. Bullets were slamming into the body of the truck, buzzing around over their heads, whining off into the sunny air.

"He's spotted us," Street said.

"Just grab the bullets and throw 'em back, hotshot," Deke said.

The truck was solid cover; two more long bursts ricocheted harmlessly off and over the three S.W.A.T. men's heads. They rose up cautiously. Hondo narrowed his eyes as he watched the figure high on the roof in the distance.

"He thinks he's got us pinned down—it'll keep him busy watching us." Hondo flipped on his walkie-talkie. "McCabe, there's a building over there a hair higher. Get up on top of it and settle in where you can get off a good shot. Move."

Across the street, out of the sniper's line of sight, T. J. crawled to the corner, stood up, and moved quickly toward the higher building on the next street, his sniper rifle held loosely as he trotted.

"Luca," Hondo went on into the walkie-talkie, "there's an open window in that building. It's across that parking lot. Work your way into position at the front edge of the lot; when we open up covering fire, take off for the window. When you get inside, go on up to the roof fast and quiet, and wait for my signal before you go out after him."

"Got it, Lieutenant," Dominic Luca said.

Across the street from where the other three S.W.A.T. men crouched behind the truck, the wiry little Italian began to crawl forward toward the open parking lot, shotgun cradled in the crook of both arms, moving ahead on his elbows. He reached the edge of the lot, peered up from cover to the parapet of the sniper's building. Luca could see the top of the man's head and the barrel of the wicked automatic rifle. He spoke low into his walkie-talkie.

"In position, Lieutenant. I can see him, so he can see me soon as I move. You better cover me good."

"We'll keep him down, Luca," Hondo replied drily. "Count five and go."

Luca counted. At the count of two, a withering fire burst from behind the truck up toward the parapet. The hail of fire raked the roof, chipping deadly stone splinters from the parapet. The sniper's head vanished.

Luca was up and running across the open parking lot.

It seemed like ten miles.

Hondo, Deke, and Street kept up their heavy fire,

19

laying down a sheet of death for anything that raised its head up over the edge of the parapet.

Luca reached the open window and dove through without stopping to look up.

The three at the truck continued their fire for another count of five, then stopped. Hondo watched the roof. The sniper's head slowly poked up; he looked around. Hondo could see the man's teeth in the sun as he laughed, raised his rifle, and began firing into the street again.

On the roof of the higher building four hundred yards away, T. J. McCabe settled into a prone firing position and sighted through his scope at the distant target roof. In the scope he had a clear view of the small, stocky sniper crouched at the edge of the parapet, empty automatic rifle clips all around him, a stack of full clips still piled beside him. T. J. set the crosswires of his scope square on the sniper's back and spoke into his walkie-talkie.

"I'm on the roof, Lieutenant," he said low. "He's clear as a coyote at dawn. I can ding him right now if you want."

Behind the truck, Hondo Harrelson watched the roof. "No, not yet, McCabe. Don't shoot him unless we have to, you got that? This one I want alive. Just stay in position, and don't let him out of your sights."

Hondo clicked off his walkie-talkie and looked at Deacon Kay. "I've got a lot of questions to ask this one. All right, move up to that parking lot."

One at a time, covering each other, Hondo, Deke, and Street dashed across the street to the far side and made their way along close to the building to the edge of the open parking lot. The sniper was busy shooting up the far end of the street, but he could spot them and open fire any second.

"Deke," Hondo snapped, "lay fire on the roof and

get us across the lot. Don't hit him, just keep his head down."

Deke nodded, took aim at the roof, and when the sniper's head showed again, opened fire. The head vanished. Hondo and Street made their dash across the parking lot to the shelter of the building line. Even if the sniper knew Hondo and Street were there below him, with Deke covering from the edge of the parking lot he couldn't lean over and fire down at anyone so close to the building without taking the chance of being instantly picked off by Deke.

Hondo and Street unhooked their grappling ropes from their S.W.A.T. belts and attached the hooks. Hondo spoke low into his walkie-talkie. "Deke, hold your position, keep his head down, but don't hit him unless you're sure we're in trouble."

Deke crouched, watching the roof. "Check, Hondo."

"McCabe," Hondo went on, "keep your scope on him. But don't ding him unless one of us is in danger or you're certain he's going to slip us."

On the far roof, T. J. nodded. "Ten-four, Lieutenant."

"Luca, report," Hondo continued.

Luca's voice was very soft. "I'm up at the head of the inside stairs at the roof door. I can hear him out there. He's sure cursing up a storm, Lieutenant."

"Cover your innocent ears," Hondo said. "We're coming up the wall. When I say the word, go out and get him, but be careful. And I want him alive."

"I'll do my best, boss," Luca said from inside the building.

Hondo nodded to Street. The two of them swung their grappling hooks, heaving them expertly up to the parapet. Both hooks caught the first time. Padded, the hooks made only dull thuds against the stone, barely noticeable above the noise of the sniper's fire still rattling in the almost empty street.

21

Hondo and Street started up, braced on the secured ropes, walking the wall as they hauled silently hand over hand, their weapons slung in front where they could fire them with one hand if they had to. Halfway up, his eyes fixed on the parapet above, Hondo Harrelson spoke quietly into the walkie-talkie hooked to his flak jacket.

"Luca, go!"

On the roof, Nicholas Cortease had just changed a clip. He was leaning over to open fire again on the wrecked hulk of the ambassador's limousine.

"Come out and take your lumps, pig!" Cortease shouted.

Then he heard the door open behind him.

Cortease whirled, his startled face a mask of surprise as he saw Dominic Luca come out the roof door. But his rifle had come up and been aimed by reflex.

"Drop it!" Luca commanded. "Get your hands—"

Cortease fired a wild burst that sailed high, and dove for the cover of a metal roof ventilator. Luca hit the dirt behind the high roof-exit housing. From there, Luca and his shotgun had half the rooftop cut off from Cortease.

"You're blocked, man!" Luca shouted. "I've got you cut from the exit! Throw down your—"

For answer, Cortease fired a long burst at the exit housing.

"Maybe you've got me blocked, pig, but I've got you pinned down!" Cortease yelled. "And you ain't gettin' no help coming out that roof door! You're gettin' no help from—"

Hondo Harrelson and Street came up over the parapet and fell behind another roof ventilator, cutting Cortease off from an escape over the rooftops.

"Yes, he is, fellow," Hondo said. "He's got a lot

22

of help, and you've got nowhere to go. Throw out the rifle."

Frantic, Cortease swivelled around on his belly until he lay behind the ventilator in a narrow wedge of cover, a tiny area of safety.

"Okay, bigshots," Cortease snarled. "You've got me pinned in, but you can't get at me—not without some of you getting blasted."

"No?" Hondo called. "Look behind you, and up a click."

Behind the ventilator, Cortease looked. He saw the distant roof and the blond head of T. J. McCabe. He saw the glint of the sun on T. J.'s rifle and scope.

"You're dead in his sights," Hondo called coldly. "You're surrounded. Come out with your hands in the air and empty."

The silence seemed to hang suspended on the sun-hot rooftop. Cortease didn't move behind his cover. Hondo showed his walkie-talkie and spoke loudly. "Okay, T. J. When I count three, kill him! One, two—"

The automatic rifle came clattering out across the roof.

"Okay! Okay!" Cortease shouted.

His hands high, he stood and stepped out from behind the ventilator. The three S.W.A.T. officers closed in on him. Hondo and Street kept him covered while Luca searched and cuffed him. Cortease looked at their flak jackets, baseball caps, and dark blue two-piece battle uniforms.

"Who the hell are you?" he said.

"Police," Hondo said.

Cortease blinked. "Police? I never saw no police that looked like you guys. Those weapons? A sniper?"

"Police from Olympic S.W.A.T.," Hondo said.

"S.W.A.T.?" Cortease said. "Yeh, I heard of you! The commando boys, the goon squad! So the pigs had

23

to call out the troopers! Well, you can't silence us, no! Our message will get out loud and clear! We'll free the oppressed peoples of the world! You hear me? We'll . . ."

Hondo Harrelson looked at the small, stocky man and slowly shook his head. It took all kinds. He turned away in disgust.

"You'll talk all right, mister—to us. Bring him!"

4

Douglas McVea switched off his car radio and pulled the small black sedan into the parking lot of an apartment building not far from the city's downtown center. He got out and walked to where another man leaned against a closed van.

"Ready, Rameri?" McVea said.

The man didn't answer, or even nod. Shorter than McVea, about the same age—mid-thirties—he was twice as wide, with heavy shoulders and thick, muscled arms. He was short-legged and barrel-chested, and his shoulders sloped down from a bull neck and a broad, flat face with small, sharp eyes that showed no expression.

"How'd it go, McVea?" the man said.

"Exactly as I said it would," McVea snapped. "It always does, remember that."

The thinnest of smiles crossed Rameri's broad face and his small eyes glittered.

"That isn't what I heard," Rameri said. "I heard Cortease killed a couple of people, shot up some cops."

"That just makes it better," McVea said. "When we hit, they'll really listen, play it careful."

"Unless Cortease talks too much. It's a murder fall now."

"He won't," McVea said, smiling. "Cortease is a fool and half crazy. He got carried away, I suppose. I figured he might do that. But he's only *half* crazy, and he's not fool enough to hang himself. He'll stick to the straight story—it's his best chance to cop a plea."

"I hope you're right," Rameri said, his hard eyes fixed on the slimmer man's arrogant face.

"I told you," McVea said, "I always am."

"You better be," Rameri said with his shark smile, looking McVea up and down slowly. "Yes sir, you really better be."

On the first floor of the Olympic Precinct, Nicholas Cortease sat in the isolated detention cell used only for the most violent and dangerous prisoners. The small, stocky man sat on the edge of the steel bunk, his face intense, his head moving back and forth in confusion. Hondo Harrelson stood against the cell bars.

"I don't know, Lieutenant, I *don't know* what happened, you know?"

Hondo was expressionless. "You're saying you don't know what you did on that roof? You're not aware of what happened out there?"

Cortease shook his head. "I remember I was—"

"A mental blackout?" Hondo said, his eyes cold and his mouth going thin. "Temporary insanity?"

"I don't know. I just—"

Hondo snorted. "No way, mister. It won't wash. You were out there after the ambassador—planned and calculated. You and your guerrilla outfit. Don't try to tell me you don't remember going up there to kill the ambassador."

25

"To kill our enemy!" Cortease shouted, jumping up. He glared at Hondo.

"So you do remember? Tell me who else—" Hondo began.

"I remember what I was doing there, sure!" Cortease began to walk up and down, intense and pacing. "I'm not apologizing! I'm proud, you hear? The Organization for the Freedom of Oppressed Peoples is going to free our people, free Palestine, free the whole oppressed world! It's a war, fuzz-man, and I'm one of the soldiers!"

"Free the world?" Hondo said. "By shooting one ambassador in a city about ten thousand miles from Palestine?"

"By shooting a hundred ambassadors, a thousand! By making all oppressors afraid to walk the streets until they take their heels off our necks! You won't stop us. You can toss me in the slammer for ten years, but you won't stop us!"

"We'll stop you in this town, Cortease," Hondo said flatly, "and murder carries a lot more than ten years."

"Killing enemies in war isn't murder, it's politics! A political action! I'm a soldier in a guerrilla war!"

Hondo watched him. "Maybe you could get away with that if you'd killed the ambassador, but you didn't. You killed ordinary citizens, innocent bystanders, and that's murder in my book."

Cortease began to shake his head back and forth again, denying and wondering at the same time.

"Yeh, you know? I mean," he went on, shaking his head like some kind of mechanical doll, "that's what I don' know. How'd I hit them people? How'd it happen? I was up there on the roof, settled in and all set, you know. Just waitin' for that pig of an ambassador. I saw the car, the limousine. Right in

26

my sights, see? When it got where I wanted it, I opened up!"

Cortease shook his head. "I ain't used to that automatic gun, it started to climb so I pulled it down. Too far. Shot out the tires, chewed up the limo engine. They piled out on the other side. I missed that goddamn ambassador. Missed!"

"Pretty bad shooting, missing at that range," Hondo said.

"Shaky, damn it, I guess," Cortease said, his head still going back and forth like a pendulum on a wire. "Missed! And I couldn't dig the ambassador out, see? I poured it on, I had to kill that fat pig! Then . . . then . . . I don't know—"

He looked up at Hondo Harrelson, his eyes wide and unbelieving. "I . . . someone screamed . . . I went crazy, yeh. . . . It was all crazy, I don' remember nothing much, you know? I just starting firin' and firin'. I mean, I was fightin' for the Cause, for freedom, and they was all the enemy down there in that street, all helping that pig ambassador! I . . ." He went on and on, shaking his head back and forth. "I just went crazy, blacked out, didn't know nothin' I was doin'."

Hondo Harrelson watched, thinking. The man just might get away with that story if he had the right jury, a good lawyer. It was a story some foreign countries might believe, and that carried weight back in Washington these days, and Washington carried weight in Sacramento. It could even be true, but . . . ?

"It won't play, Cortease. Not with me," Hondo said, pushing the small man.

"I'm a soldier, Lieutenant. Political."

"Cortease isn't any Arab name," Hondo said.

"Who says we're all Arabs? Lots of different guys are in our group, fightin' for the oppressed peoples. Hell, our leader ain't no Arab, he's an Irish—"

27

Cortease caught himself, stopped, glared defiantly up at Harrelson.

"An Irishman? That's hard to believe," Hondo said.

"Believe it. We got lots of old IRA men."

"What's his name?"

Cortease laughed. "Don't get cute, fuzz-man. Name, rank, and serial number. I'm a soldier, right?"

"He sent you on a suicide job."

"Every job is suicide for us."

"The freedom fighter," Hondo said.

"You got it," Cortease said. "A political prisoner, that's what I am."

"Nuts," Hondo Harrelson said. He walked to the john in the detention cell, sat down, leaned back, and stared at Cortease. "You're a two-bit, small-time crook. We ran your name through the computer, Cortease. You've got a rap sheet a mile long, and all nickel-and-dime. Assault, robbery, street heists, a couple of dismissals on grand theft and auto theft. Just a born gorilla, not guerrilla. Now you better tell me what's going on, or you'll spend a long time in the slam."

"Throw away the key, go ahead," Cortease said, "but you're talkin' about the old Nick Cortease. Sure, I was a nothin' punk. Only that was before I got the word, fuzz-man, saw the true light. I got me a Cause now, and I'm a soldier."

"For the same group that's been phoning in warnings to the police all week?"

"Got you sweatin', Lieutenant?" Cortease sneered.

"No, but they've got me wondering. A lot of talk for the shooting of one ambassador—and a missed shot, at that."

"Just keep wondering, fuzz," Cortease said.

"One message said, 'First a scratch, a cut, and then

the mortal blow.' I think you and the ambassador is the cut. What's the mortal blow, Cortease?"

"I don' know what you're talkin' about," Cortease said.

"I think you do know," Hondo said.

Cortease laughed nastily. "Well, maybe I do, maybe I don't. And maybe you'll find out, right?"

Hondo watched the man again for a moment. Then he got up and rattled the bars for the guard. As the guard came to let him out, he turned once more to Nicholas Cortease.

"Talk, and maybe it'd go easier on you."

Cortease laughed. "Sweat, fuzz, sweat!"

"We'll both sweat a little, I guess," Hondo said as he left the cell, "but you're going to have a lot longer time to sweat in, mister. The charge is murder one."

Hondo walked out and along the silent precinct corridor. Behind him Cortease was yelling: "I'll tell you this, fuzz, it'll blow your mind! You hear? It's big, fuzz-man, real big!"

Harrelson closed the corridor door, scowling.

5

The new downtown Sports Arena was a giant domed structure set in the center of vast black-top parking lots. Built in a razed section of what had once been the city's worst slum, it was still surrounded by the gaudy neon signs of the city's nightclub district. Lines of fans were already gathered at the ticket windows buying seats for tonight's big basketball game.

None of the avid hoop devotees noticed the unmarked van that pulled up to the arena's service entrance. Two men got out of the van and began to unload camera equipment. One was the leanly handsome Douglas McVea. The other was the heavy Joseph Rameri. They briskly went about the job of getting out the motion picture equipment and loading it onto dollies.

Inside the arena, the city's championship team—the Owls—were sweating and slamming through a hard pregame scrimmage. As the giants pounded up and down the hardwood floor, a smaller man emerged suddenly from the pack to leap higher than the giants and almost effortlessly intercept the ball. A lithe, athletically graceful man in his late twenties, he drove in hard to the basket, left three bigger men flatfooted, and sank a classic lay-up.

There was a smattering of applause from some of the favored few in the empty stands who had the clout to be allowed to sit in on a scrimmage.

"Go, Ollie!"

" 'Atsa way, Ollie!"

Ollie Wyatt, the Owls' All-League, high-scoring guard took a small bow and stood grinning and breathing lightly in center court. Pete Morgan, the coach of the Owls, stood in his sweatsuit with his hands on his hips, not applauding.

"Swell," Morgan said to his hard-breathing team. "As pretty a steal and fast break as I ever saw—and about the lousiest passing and defense. Keep it up, and you'll make Ollie a millionaire at contract time! I wish the Bisons would be so nice to him. If we can't stop Ollie in a scrimmage, or at least make him sweat a little for a basket, we won't be stopping the Bisons tonight. Now let's get the goddamned lead out, okay? Ollie, take ten. Benson, you and Sam—"

Ollie Wyatt trotted to the training table, took a

pull on the water bottle, spat it out. As he picked up a ball and began practicing double-dribbling with both hands in front of an extra basket on the side, a tall, well-dressed woman walked up to him. In her late twenties, she had the face of an ex-model and the manner of an executive vice president.

"Ollie," she said crisply, "you got my message about that photo session today?"

"Sure did, Miss Phillips," the star guard said. He did a few fancy dribbling steps, passed the ball from hand to hand behind his back, and laid it up and into the side basket with a textbook fall-away jump shot. "Only just remember, no nude centerfolds, okay? My fox, she don't dig sharing the view."

There was a snicker or two from his teammates out on the floor. Pete Morgan roared, "Ollie can make jokes, you clowns, he knows how to play basketball! The next guy I catch with his mind not one-hundred-and-sixty percent on this scrimmage gets to sit out the next two games! Now, play number six! Move!"

Miss Phillips just sighed. "No nudes, Ollie. They didn't even ask, sorry. And can't you make it Robin? I'm just the public-relations lady, not the company president."

"You're front office, I'm just a jock." Ollie grinned.

"You mean I'm not a jock," Robin Phillips said. "I can't even wear a jock, right?"

"Sorry, I guess I'm still not used to ladies around here," Ollie Wyatt said. "Maybe they'll ask *you* to pose nude? Maybe I'll ask you my—"

Robin Phillips shook her head. "Never mind, clown, go play basketball. I'll call you for the photo session."

Ollie rejoined the team out in center court, his grin fading at once, all serious and intent on what Pete Morgan was telling the team. Robin Phillips watched him for a moment, an approving smile on her face. Ollie was a nice guy—and a hell of a good basketball player.

Then her eyes spotted the dollies of camera equipment coming in at the far end of the arena. She hurried around the basketball court to where Douglas McVea and Joseph Rameri were shepherding the cameras, stands, and coils of cable. McVea saw her approaching.

"Miss Phillips," he said, smiling pleasantly, "this is my cameraman Joseph Rameri."

Robin Phillips nodded. "Nice to meet you, Mr. Rameri."

"Sure," the heavy-faced man said, "my pleasure."

McVea said, "We can't tell you how much we appreciate your cooperation on the film. Rameri's wanted a chance to shoot a real basketball team in action for years."

"You can say that again," Rameri said, grinning at McVea. "I never shot a whole basketball team."

"Don't mention it," Robin Phillips said briskly. "Your documentary will help us sell tickets, and that's what I get paid for. And as long as we'll be working together for a time, my name's Robin. Makes it a lot easier."

"Robin it is," McVea said with an elegant bow. "And I'm Doug. I think this will be a pleasure all around."

"I hope so," Robin Phillips said. "Now, is there anything special I can help you with?"

"I don't believe so, not at the moment," McVea said.

"No, thanks," Rameri said as he picked up a hand-held 35-mm. camera from the dolly. "I'll just go take some stills. It'll help me line up my shots when we start shooting the flick."

"Well," Robin began, "I can help get the players—"

The public-address system began to boom out

32

through the arena: *"Phone call, Robin Phillips . . . Miss Phillips, phone—"*

Robin Phillips nodded to McVea and Rameri. "Excuse me, I'll be right back. You just go ahead. I've alerted the players and Coach Morgan."

She hurried off toward the front office. McVea and Rameri watched her go. McVea seemed to be undressing her with hot eyes. Rameri, uninterested, turned quickly back to the basketball court. Then he saw the look in McVea's eyes. His heavy mouth curled in a sneer; his flat little eyes fixed on McVea. He looked like a tiger sizing up its dinner.

"You got too many things on your mind, McVea," the muscleman said. "Too many hangups to be good at this kind of work."

"You don't like women, Rameri?" McVea snapped.

"Take 'em or leave 'em," Rameri said. "A man got to have one sometimes, sure. So take one and good-bye."

"You must do very well," McVea said.

"I ain't had no complaints."

"Tell me more later," McVea said. "Right now we better get to work."

"Make with the watch-the-birdie?" Rameri said. "Okay, what do you want me to shoot? With the camera, I mean."

"Everything in the arena. Not the people, except for cover. The whole interior. We're going to have to know the security layout and the floor plan below the stands—especially the setup down there around the home locker room. Get a fix on all the exits, which ones we can use best, which ones we can seal off. And cover the area *around* all the exits too."

"Piece of cake," Rameri said. "I'll get a fix on every spot anyone could lay for us on the getaway."

"Nice and easy, careful and all that. That's the way we want it."

"Well," Rameri said, licking his heavy lips, "maybe we don't want it *too* easy. I didn't sign up for this caper just to shoot pictures, now did I? I mean, any cameraman could handle that."

"We want it as easy as it can be!" McVea said harshly, glaring at Rameri. "That's not how a guerrilla unit works, you understand? We don't want to kill anyone we don't have to. You get your kicks some other time!"

"Sure, no one killed we don't have to kill," Rameri said softly, his voice almost stroking the air, his eyes with the same look McVea's eyes had when he looked at women. "But in a caper like this, a big blow for the Cause, someone's sure to try bein' a hero, and—".

McVea stared at the massive man. "Maybe you should think more about women, Rameri. Maybe it's healthier."

"You think about women, pretty man," Rameri said coldly.

McVea nodded. "Okay, but we've both got a job here. A big job. We don't want any slips. The Organization for the Freedom of Oppressed Peoples shoots only its real enemies, remember that. We shoot oppressors, not little people like ourselves. We've got to keep a clean image, you got that?"

"I got it, McVea, but I ain't so sure I like it," Rameri said. "I ain't so sure I want to go with a gang of tin soldiers. I ain't so sure I like bein' so cute about it."

"Be sure, or get out. Now! Or stay, and remember who's giving the orders in this unit!"

McVea's voice was sharp as he stared at Rameri. The other man stared back. They stood, surrounded by the noise and pounding feet of the Sports Arena, like two tomcats facing off in some back alley. Then Rameri shrugged.

"So when do we go?" he said.

"When I say we do!" McVea said. Then he nodded. "Soon. The warning messages have all been delivered; the rest of the team is ready. Cortease should have them sitting on nails by now. I'd say . . . tonight."

Rameri licked his lips again, his thick nostrils flaring. He almost breathed the word.

"Tonight!"

6

In the Emergency Command room of Olympic S.W.A.T., Hondo Harrelson sat on the edge of a planning table and watched his men. Deacon Kay was studying the operations map of the city on the E.C. wall. Jim Street sat in a chair tilted against the same wall. They all looked concerned, uneasy.

"Well, that's Cortease's story," Hondo said.

T. J. McCabe was cleaning his sniper rifle, examining it closely. Dominic Luca was trying to work one of those puzzles in which small steel balls have to be rolled into holes on a flat surface. Luca wasn't having much luck with it.

"Everybody's crazy," Luca said.

Jim Street said, "You believe Cortease, Lieutenant? I mean, he doesn't seem much like an Arab terrorist to me."

"Not a terrorist," Hondo said, "a soldier—freeing the oppressed peoples of the world."

Deke Kay turned from the operations map. "He's got a rap sheet back to when he was a teen-ager.

Nothing big, but awful busy, and all of it right here in town."

"That doesn't sound like the last of the big-time Arab terrorists to me," T. J. said, working linseed oil into the stock of his rifle.

"I know," Hondo agreed, "but that's what he says he is. I interrogated him for three hours, off and on, and he swears it's a whole new Nick Cortease we've got. He was out to kill that ambassador. He says he was just a petty crook once, but now he's found a Cause."

"He's found a one-way ticket to the laughing academy, if you ask me," Luca said, abandoning his puzzle. "I figure he was nuts before he ever got on that roof, Lieutenant. I'll bet he doesn't even belong to a terrorist gang, he's just a lone dingbat."

"You think he had those pamphlets printed up by himself?" Deke wanted to know.

"And what about those phone warnings?" Street added.

"Okay, maybe there is a two-bit group," Luca said, "but what can a bunch of crackpots like that do?"

"Do?" Hondo said. He turned toward Deke Kay. "Deke, set it up and roll it."

Deke placed a small movie projector on a table at the rear of the E.C. room. He pressed a button somewhere under the table, and a screen slid down on the far wall. Deke flicked a switch on the movie projector, and it began to roll.

"Wow!" T. J. exclaimed.

Wild gunfire exploded on the screen. Men ran and dove for cover in lush, parkline grounds. The Olympic flag flew over a concrete barracks building. Heavily armed men could be seen at the windows of the barracks, trading shattering volleys with hordes of uniformed policemen out on the grounds.

"Man," Luca breathed, "it looks like World War II."

The holocaust on the screen shifted angles, and armed policemen in dark combat uniforms and flak jackets were seen swarming up walls and fire escapes to a roof next to the besieged barracks. The police began pouring fire down into the building.

Hondo Harrelson hadn't moved from the edge of the table in the darkened room. He watched the battle on the screen. . . .

Captain Walter Dawson crouched in the outside stairwell across the street from the slum tenement. "City Hall says no deals, we go in and get them," he said. Young Dan Harrelson nodded. "Hell, what can they do? A bunch of crazy crackpots. They'll cut and run the first time they see us moving in." Dawson nodded, but chewed on a fingernail, uncertain. "Yeh, sure, Harrelson, but that's an awful big open area to cross to get at that cellar. Maybe we should get up on the roof, work down inside. Kick in the cellar door and surprise them." Dan Harrelson said, "We could put a sniper or two up on the roof of this building, shoot in the cellar windows, and keep them back from the windows." Dawson shrugged. "We don't have anyone who can shoot that good, and no rifles with us anyway. No, we—" A patrolman said, "Captain, look! . . ."

On the small movie screen the picture jumped and flickered in the darkened E.C. room. The foreign policemen on the lush grounds and up on the adjoining roof stopped firing. Some of them half stood to get a better look. On a balcony of the surrounded barracks two hooded gunmen held three blindfolded hostages in front of them. They held guns to the heads of the hostages. The firing ceased; the attacking policemen all looking at each other, and at their leaders, for instructions.

. . . *Captain Dawson cursed. "Damn and hell, they've got a couple of hostages!" In the doorway to the tenement cellar, an old man and a scrawny slum kid held their guns in the backs of two pale, shaking citizens. A patrolman said, "What do we do now, Captain?" Young Dan Harrelson said, "We'll get around to the rear, break in, and grab them while they're all up front. They won't do anything, won't even know what hit them." Captain Dawson hesitated. "I don't know, I don't—"*

"Fanatics," T. J. muttered, watching the screen in the E.C. room. "You can't trust 'em or figure 'em."

"They believe they're doing right," Jim Street said, "and they're ready to die for the Cause. Brave and determined."

The picture flickered sharply, and it was early evening. The policemen stood around the side entrance of the barracks, their weapons ready but lowered. The masked terrorists came out the side entrance warily, each with a blindfolded hostage in front of him. They climbed into a bus. Weapons jutting from all its windows, the blindfolded hostages sitting helpless, the bus rolled away.

"There!" Deke said sharply. "They could have hit them there, when the bus had to slow for the turn out of the barracks driveway. They should have tried it there and then."

"I don't know," Street said. He shook his head. "A big risk."

The picture jumped again, and the bus was speeding along an airport runway, slowing as it came close to a waiting jet. It was night now on the screen as the S.W.A.T. team watched. The images leaped and jerked, the whole picture tilting and jumping violently as firing erupted all across the night airfield.

Suddenly, shots sounded clear from inside the stopped bus. There was a silence on the screen. Three more shots from inside the bus. Then two figures jumped out and half ran and half staggered off to collapse on the runway as the whole bus exploded in a sheet of flame that leaped up into the night sky, outlining all the milling, running, staring shadows on the airfield.

. . . *"I don't know,"* Captain Dawson said. *"If we rush them they could kill those hostages, get some of us. Damn it, I can handle crooks, muggers, but these fanatics, these damned political people—"* Young Dan Harrelson said, *"We've got to teach these Reds they can't get away with it."* Captain Dawson looked at him. *"Teach them? How do we do that, Harrelson?"*

On the small screen the bus burned fiercely on the airfield. No one else came out—no hostages, and no Arabs except the two already dead on the runway. The police walked slowly toward the shattered bus that was only a burning coffin now.

"Deke," Hondo said.

Deke Kay turned on the lights, switched off the projector. The screen rose silently back into the ceiling of the E.C. room. Quiet as it was sliding back up, it could be heard faintly in the heavy silence of the E.C. room. Hondo still sat on the edge of his table watching them all, but no one said anything. Each was thinking his own thoughts about what he'd just seen on the screen.

Hondo picked up one of the pamphlets Nicholas Cortease had thrown from the roof and read aloud. "The Organization for the Freedom of Oppressed Peoples—Red September, the hour of retribution is near!"

He put the pamphlet down, looked at each of his men in turn. Deacon Kay was nodding, his face serious, as if he were filing the words away to be remembered—a long-time cop. Jim Street seemed to be evaluating the words, judging their truth and importance, trying to understand who had written them. Luca was shaking his head, unable to figure out who'd written the pamphlet or who'd even want to. T. J. went on cleaning his rifle.

"They can do plenty more than talk," Hondo said. "You've seen it. That's the way The Organization for the Freedom of Oppressed Peoples operates. They're ready to kill, and, as Street said, they're more than ready to die for their Cause."

He looked down at the pamphlet. " 'The hour of retribution is near.' A warning, a threat. Terrorists of the worst kind. You saw it on the screen. Even though the authorities in Munich tried to negotiate with them, tried to trade a safe escape for the hostage's lives, the offer wasn't enough for the terrorists. And you saw what happened. Eight dead."

"But," T. J. said suddenly, looking up, "that was ten thousand miles away!"

"And it can't happen here, eh?" Hondo said. He seemed to look inside himself. "Eight dead. When I was just starting out on the L.A.P.D. we had—"

He stopped, shook his head as if to clear it. Deke Kay watched him. He was the only one there who knew anything about that violent siege long ago in the slums of Los Angeles. Deke looked a little worried as he watched his chief. Hondo took a deep breath.

"Well," he said, "we've been lucky so far, but it *can* happen here, believe me. According to Nick Cortease, it's *going* to happen here—and soon. Only it's not, because we're going to see to it that it doesn't."

"Hell," Luca said, "I just don't believe that Cortease crum."

"Neither do I," T. J. echoed.

"You know," Street said, "Cortease gave up awful easy. Those terrorists on the screen didn't give up—they didn't let anyone take them alive."

Hondo nodded. "I've thought about that. I've thought about him missing the ambassador, too. Maybe there is something different going on, but some terrorists do give up when cornered."

"If it was all some kind of phony trick," Deke Kay said, "Cortease sure went to a lot of trouble shooting up the countryside, taking an almost sure murder rap."

"And we can't take a chance anyway," Hondo said. "Those pamphlets are real enough, and the warning calls we've been getting all week sounded real. Everything points to the terrorists getting ready for a big hit. What we don't know is where and when, and that's what we're going to work to find out."

"How, Hondo?" Jim Street asked.

"By being ready for anything—and checking every possibility we can think of that would make a big, world-news-making demonstration," Hondo said. He looked toward Deke. "Get a list of every banquet room in town that can hold over three hundred people, and find out what functions are going on in them in the next week. Who's having banquets, why, all that."

"Roger," Deke said.

Hondo turned to the other three. "The four of us will split up, check out all the public parks, arenas, theaters, major hotels, the race track, political rallies —any place at all a terrorist group might find a target big enough to get international attention if it was hit."

T. J. whistled. "That's a lot of ground, Lieutenant."

"And not much time," Hondo said, "so we better get moving."

7

T. J. McCabe had checked out the football stadium and two hotels by the time he got to the Sports Arena. Nothing big was scheduled at any of the first three places for the next two weeks. T. J. had asked to cover the Sports Arena, and when his business was finished, he'd learned only what he already knew—that the Owls had a home game tonight and another in two days, and that the Polar Bears, the hockey team, were on the road all week. He walked out into the empty stands above the arena floor.

T. J. sat down halfway up the rows of empty seats and watched the scrimmage on the court. As T. J. watched, Ollie Wyatt broke away from the pack, outraced three pursuers, and sank a leaping dunk that took him high above the rim, short though he was for a basketball player. T. J. grinned, applauding vigorously.

On the floor, Ollie Wyatt left the court to grab a towel and idly glanced up toward the sound of the knowledgeable clapping. T. J. gave a small wave and a smile. Ollie broke into a broad grin, tossed his towel away, and walked up into the stands to where T. J. was sitting.

"T. J., man, hey, how're you doing?" Ollie cried.

"Hi, Ollie," T. J. said. "Great to see you again."

"Yeh?" Ollie said, stepping back. "So how come you got to hide up here in the stands? Too big a man on the fuzz now to come around and talk to an old friend?"

T. J. reddened and shrugged bashfully. "You know better than that, Ollie. I just figured you were busy. I mean, you're a big star, and down there with the team, and . . ." He trailed off lamely.

"You mean you think *I'm* too big to talk to an old buddy?" Ollie said. "Hey, man, I oughta whomp you one for that. You figure I got me a case of fat head?"

"Hell, no, Ollie," T. J. protested. "I mean, well, I was here on business, and I just figured to take a break, and . . . Aw, gee, it's good to talk to you, Ollie."

"Like the old days in high school?"

"Good old days," T. J. said.

"You know it, buddy," Ollie said quietly. "Hey, tell you what. I'll be finished sweating here in a couple minutes, and then I'm free till game time. I'll get Joanne, and we'll have some elegant groceries. Okay?"

"That'd be great," T. J. said, "only I'm on duty. Got to check in at the precinct."

"So okay, I'll check in with you," Ollie said. "Always did want to see that storm-trooper HQ of yours." He grinned. "Only kidding, old buddy. You just sit right here, send your paddy wagon home, and *I'll* drive you to the fuzz place."

"The lieutenant is picking me up."

"Call the lieutenant off," Ollie insisted. "I'm not letting you out of my sight."

T. J. laughed, and as Ollie returned to the court he went out to a pay phone and called the S.W.A.T. war room. Hondo Harrelson was there. T. J. told him not to bother to pick him up, that Ollie Wyatt would bring him back.

"The Owls' Ollie Wyatt? Himself?" Hondo said.

"We're kind of old friends," T. J. explained.

"T. J., you're a constant surprise to me," Hondo said.

Smiling to himself over having impressed Hondo with his friendship with Ollie Wyatt, T. J. went back to his seat in the stands to watch the end of the scrimmage session. As he did, his smile slowly faded, and he sighed to himself. Ollie was beautiful to watch when he moved on a basketball court—totally at home, totally in control. It was Ollie's world, and once it had been T. J.'s world too. He'd been good, he knew that, but how good? Could he have made it in professional ball like Ollie? Maybe he couldn't have been as good as Ollie, not many guys were, but could he have played pro ball? He didn't know, and never would now. He liked the work he'd chosen, being a special cop and part of the growing S.W.A.T. organization. Still . . . ? It would have been nice to know if he could have made it as a pro.

"You could've made it, but maybe what you're doing's more important."

T. J. jerked out of his reverie. "What? Oh, Ollie. Ready?"

"I know that look, man," Ollie Wyatt said quietly. "Being a pro ball player's fun, but maybe it's not so real, you know? I mean, sometimes I wonder about grown men still playing a game for a living. Come on, let's get you checked in, and then we'll pick up my frau and get some grub."

Ollie led the way down under the stands and past the Owls' locker room. He and T. J. almost walked into two men with a dolly-load of camera and recording equipment. One of them, a massive, bull-like man, was taking still shots of the locker room area. The taller and smoother of the two smiled at Ollie.

"Don't forget to come back soon, Wyatt," Douglas

44

McVea said. "We can't shoot a documentary of the Owls without their biggest star."

"I just play ball," Ollie said. "The buildup's not my department. You makin' out okay?"

"Just fine," Joseph Rameri said, snapping another shot of the corridor outside the locker room. "We're makin' out just fine."

"But you hurry back, Mr. Wyatt," McVea said, grinning at T. J. "You're very important to us."

T. J. looked at the equipment, and then up and down the empty corridor. "Just what are you guys doing? Why shoot an empty corridor?"

"They're making a documentary," Ollie Wyatt said. "One of our P.R. lady's brainstorms. Anything to sell tickets."

"We're just setting our angles, planning our continuity," McVea explained. "Sort of a map for the real thing."

"So when do we see the real thing?" Ollie asked.

"Soon," Rameri said, snapping a shot of T. J. and Ollie. He grinned. "Real soon."

"Well, we'll leave you to it, man," Ollie said.

Out in the parking lot T. J. gaped at the fire-engine-red Maserati as Ollie climbed behind the wheel.

"Get in, wise guy," Ollie said, "and take a good look at it—it may be its last ride. My fox says family men don't drive Maseratis, and my manager says family men can't afford 'em."

Ollie drove with the same verve and lightning sharp reflexes that made him such a terror on a basketball court. In less than ten minutes they pulled into the parking lot of Olympic Precinct, and T. J. took Ollie up to the E.C. room on the second floor. Deacon, Street, and Luca all exchanged unbelieving but impressed glances as T. J. and Ollie walked in. Hondo came in from his office.

"Ollie," T. J. said, "this is Lieutenant Harrelson."

"Lieutenant," Ollie said, shaking hands.

"Pleasure meeting you, Ollie," Hondo said. "I've sees you lay in a couple of thousand points, college and professional."

"And I've got the bruises for every one of them," Ollie said.

T. J. introduced the others. "This is Deke Kay, Jim Street, and Dom Luca. Meet Ollie Wyatt, guys."

They all shook hands.

"T. J.'s always telling us about you two being buddies," Street said. "Playing ball together, and all that. I guess I never really believed it before."

"I mean, old Dudley Do-Right there and the great Ollie Wyatt playing on the same court? Crazy," Luca said.

"Don't you go downgrading T. J.," Ollie said, shaking his head. "He was a pretty fair country ball player, you better believe it."

"Hell," T. J. said. "In the school we went to, everyone played ball."

"Listen to him," Ollie said. "Now you're going to give us that modest jive, are you? Someday we're going to have to show them old 'Whistle One.'"

Ollie gave a shrill whistle in two sharp blasts. Hondo and the other S.W.A.T. men looked at both Ollie and T. J. curiously.

"It's a special play we worked out for our high school championship game," T. J. started to explain. "See, we'd lay five guys out on the floor, and then—"

"Hey, man," Ollie broke in, "I came to take you to dinner, remember? My old lady's eating for two right now. She'll be starved if we don't get by soon."

Hondo said, "I'm sorry, Ollie, but we can't spare T. J. right now. We're in the middle of something. You have anything to report, T. J.?"

46

"Not a thing, Lieutenant. Hotels, football stadium, and Sports Arena all look quiet."

Ollie said, "Then I'm gonna make you take a raincheck, T. J. We'll be back in town in a couple weeks. Let's say—"

"A couple of weeks?" T. J. said, dismayed. "Gee—"

"Change your mind," Ollie said quickly. "Look, you have to eat. Nothing fancy. Some beer and chili."

"Beer and chili?" Deacon said. "Right before a game?"

"Hey, man," Ollie laughed, "that's what makes us so mean."

T. J. glanced at Hondo.

"All right, go ahead. As the man said, you have to eat," Hondo said.

"Why don't you join us, Lieutenant?" Ollie invited.

"Well, I can't make dinner, but I'll join you for some coffee, thanks."

"How about Crazy Mary's, Ollie?" T. J. said. "It's right around the corner."

"You got it," Ollie said. "Six o'clock. My old lady'll be glad to meet you, Lieutenant. She thinks cops are important."

They all laughed as Ollie turned to leave. Hondo stopped him.

"Ollie, since you're here, have you noticed anything suspicious around the Sports Arena lately?"

"Nothing but some teams playing us better than they should."

Luca said, "Maybe that's it. The terrorists are disguised as basketball players. They're gonna ruin the league."

T. J. said, "I did run into two guys making a movie about the Owls. A documentary, they said. Only . . . well, I don't know, but there *was* something funny about them."

"How funny?" Hondo said.

T. J. frowned. "I'm not sure, Lieutenant. I mean, they had all the equipment, but they didn't *sound* like movie men."

"Hey, they're just making a documentary flick, T. J." Ollie said. "What do you want, C. B. De-Mille?"

"You know these people, Ollie?" Hondo asked.

"Sure, our P.R. lady brought them in," Ollie said. "I guess she figures a movie'll sell some tickets. P.R. people are always cluttering up the place on a pro team. It's a pain, but I guess it does help the box office. Well, I better go pick up my frau. See you at six."

The basketball star left with a wave to them all. When he was gone, Hondo faced his men.

"Well? Anything suspicious anywhere?"

They all shook their heads.

"Damn," Hondo scowled. "Something's going to happen, I feel it. But when—and where?"

They all looked at each other in the heavy silence of the E.C. room.

8

On the third floor of an old apartment building downtown near the Sports Arena, a hard-faced black man got out of the elevator. His sharp, experienced eyes swept the deserted corridor. He was in his thirties, and he had the scars above his eyes and crisscrossing his left cheek to prove that they had been thirty hard years.

Satisfied that the third-floor corridor held no immediate danger, the man nodded, and a second man stepped from the elevator. Younger, in his twenties, the second man had an even-featured face with no scars and eyes full of eager bravado. He imitated the older black man's survey of the corridor and tried to show the same cool hardness, but the nervous excitement in his eyes betrayed his lack of experience.

"Man," the black said, "you looks, but you don't see nothin'. This ain't no game, Burke. Don't try to be what you ain't yet—it gets in the way of learning."

"Get off my back, Forrester," the young man said.

"You got off that elevator like you had an audience, sonny," the black man said. "You ain't lookin', you're posing like people was watchin' you. Ain't no one watchin', ain't no one cares how tough you are, ain't no one gonna see you except someone you don't want to see you—someone you better see first and hope don't see you at all."

Burke reddened, clenched his fists, glared at Forrester. He took a step toward the black man, who just stood there silently. Burke blinked, licked his lips.

"You better stop ridin' me, Forrester."

Forrester curled his lip. "Son, I'll ride you all day as long as we're in this thing. My hide depends on what you do, and my hide means a lot to me. You got that?"

"Okay, okay!" Burke said, backing away. "I ain't gonna make no mistakes. You'll see."

"You'll be the first man I ever knew who didn't," Forrester said drily. "Just hang loose—remember we ain't makin' no TV show. This is for real, boy. Now come on."

The black man led the way down the silent corridor to the fourth door. He stood and listened for a moment, his eyes automatically checking the corridor once more. Then he knocked—two short, a long, and a short. A voice came from behind the door: "Who is it?"

"Message from Cairo," Forrester said.

"Who in Cairo?"

"The sheik himself," Forrester said.

The apartment door clicked and opened, and Forrester and Burke went inside. The door closed sharply behind them. Burke whirled to face Joseph Rameri, who leaned against the closed door. The massive, cold-faced Rameri smiled at Burke's jumpiness. Forrester hadn't even glanced around when the door closed. He knew who was in the room, and which sounds and actions meant danger and which didn't.

"Hello, Rameri," was all he said, not turning.

It was an ordinary apartment, small and compact, with plain furniture that looked worn but not much used, as if no one really lived in the apartment. The walls weren't ordinary. They were covered from one end to the other with large, blown-up still photos— photos of key parts of the Sports Arena a few blocks away. There were shots of bolted exit doors, security alarms, guards' phone posts and clock-ins, staircases, the entrance to and interior of the locker room, and dozens of shots of the arena's vast interior taken from every possible angle.

Douglas McVea stood in front of the rows of photographs. He smiled at the two newcomers as Forrester and Burke gaped at the pictures.

"It's funny," McVea said, enjoying himself. "You start aiming cameras, and all the doors in the world start opening up for you." He laughed aloud. "Everybody wants to be in a movie."

Joseph Rameri had left the door and was seated at a long table cleaning one of four automatic rifles. He handled the deadly weapon lovingly, almost cradling it against his barrel chest, stroking the hard blue metal.

"Other things open doors, too," he said.

"Not as many, Rameri, and not as easily," McVea said.

Rameri looked up, his small eyes flat. "I'm not interested in *all* the doors in the world opening up, you know? Just in the *right* doors."

"We all are, aren't we?" McVea said. "You'd kick them in, blow them down. Easy enough—but maybe it's not so easy to get out through those same doors that way."

Rameri swung the automatic rifle around the small room and brought it to rest aimed straight at McVea's chest. He wasn't smiling.

"I'd get in, and I'd get out," Rameri said. "Anyone got in my way . . . bingo!"

"Dead bodies, and nothing accomplished," McVea said. "You know, Rameri, you're a lucky man—you've got me to do the thinking for you."

The two stared at each other. The small room was silent. Burke licked his lips again. Forrester's dark face was enigmatic, but his eyes were wary, uneasy.

Rameri squeezed the trigger of the rifle aimed at McVea's chest. It clicked sharply on the empty chamber.

"Bingo," Rameri said softly.

McVea was pale. "Without me, this strike gets nowhere. Remember that, Rameri."

"Sure, bright boy," Rameri said lightly. "It's your brain-baby—just as long as you get us that million-dollar payoff you talk about. For the Cause, right?"

"For the Cause," McVea said just as lightly, "but, sorry, not a million."

"Not a—" Burke began.

"You told us—" Forrester broke in.

Rameri was up, his voice deadly. "A million is what you said, it's what you promised. You better—"

"So I lie a lot," McVea said. He smiled. "We're

not going to ask for a million—we're going to ask for *two* million!"

He looked at them all. "And we're going to get it."

"Hey, great!" Burke cried.

Forrester laughed too. "That's good arithmetic, Mc-Vea."

"But lousy vibes," Rameri snapped, glaring at McVea. "Don't play cute little tricks with me, bright baby. When you got new plans, you tell us, you hear?"

"I don't want to confuse your brain, Rameri," Mc-Vea said.

"You listen—" Rameri began, stepping toward Mc-Vea.

Forrester swore. "Damn it, we all got a job to do! Me, I didn't sign to risk my hide while you two play kid games with each other. We all got our part—let's do it."

McVea nodded. "He's right. We don't have much time. We better start getting the bombs ready."

"I'll drink to that," Rameri said.

The four of them gathered around a long table. McVea and Forrester lifted a heavy suitcase up onto the table, opened it, and began to take out wires, caps, and blocks of plastic explosive.

In the best corner booth in Crazy Mary's, Hondo Harrelson sat back with his cup of coffee and watched the younger people eat their chili. Hondo was tired. It had been a long, frustrating day with nothing to prove his hunch that the terrorists were about to strike somewhere near, and soon. Maybe he was wrong, maybe the terrorists weren't going to strike again, had shot their bolt with the abortive attack by Cortease on the ambassador. The high spirits of the others were making him feel better.

". . . And then the Owls made me an offer,"

Ollie Wyatt was saying, "but I said 'no way' unless this foxy little lady comes with me."

He moved closer to his wife, gave her a squeeze. She smiled, punched him lightly on the arm.

"Blackmail," Joanne Wyatt said. "What could I do? I was an Owl fan."

She was a bright, pretty, appealing girl in her twenties, normally slim and lithe, but over seven months pregnant now. Their obvious love for each other, and for the coming baby, was apparent in every look and touch. They touched each other often.

"The only thing was," she went on, "I still had another year to go in college for my master's degree, and I wasn't about to give that up for any itinerant basketball player."

Ollie and Hondo laughed.

"Good girl, Joanne," T. J. said, grinning.

"That's my old lady," Ollie said, nodding. "She still hits like Muhammed Ali."

Hondo said, "I'd say that Ollie isn't doing too bad. For an 'itinerant basketball player,' that is."

"Well . . ." Joanne said in mock doubt, "I guess his prospects have brightened up a little—for a little man."

They all laughed again.

"But it still took the team's general manager to talk her into marrying me," Ollie declared.

"That's so." Joanne nodded. "He sure talked a good game, that G.M. I almost told him to start speaking for himself."

Then, as if to prove what a ridiculous idea that was, Joanne moved closer to Ollie and gave him a quick, light kiss.

"So now you know the truth," Ollie said. "Behind every team's top scorer, there's always a foxy little lady—*pushing*. Score more points, she's just seen this big new house we can't live without! She's just seen this beautiful new car—score more points! She's just seen—"

"Ollie!" Joanne cried, and punched him on the arm.

Ollie ducked away in mock fear. "Just kidding, honey, just kidding! Without you inspiring me, I'm nothing."

"And *that's* the truth," Joanne said.

Ollie grinned, turning to T. J. "You're comin' to the game tonight, old buddy, right? I've got the tickets for you both."

"Hey, great!" T. J. exclaimed.

He looked eagerly at Hondo, and his happiness faded. The lieutenant shook his head.

"We'd like to, Ollie, but we'll have to take a raincheck," Hondo said. "The whole team's on ready-alert status tonight, and that means we all sit by a phone with our hands out."

"Hey, that's too bad," Ollie said, smiling. "And me with a hunch I'm going to blow the arena apart tonight."

"Don't worry," Hondo said, "I'm going to be at a phone right in front of the TV set, and I think T. J. will be too."

"You believe it, buddy," T. J. said to Ollie.

"And you better eat up, honey," Joanne said, "or you'll do all your scoring in the second half."

"See what I mean?" Ollie said. "Pushing, always pushing!"

"Well, I don't have a bet down on the Bisons, dear," Joanne said.

They laughed and dug into their chili. Hondo sipped his coffee, watching them with a smile. Maybe he really was wrong, maybe there would be no trouble. He felt a lot better. After all, they were a long way from Israel or Egypt.

In the small apartment near the Sports Arena the men sat back around the long table. Four assembled time bombs lay in front of them. Beside the bombs, a blueprint of the Sports Arena was spread flat. Next to that, the four automatic rifles lay assembled. Joseph Rameri was polishing the last front sight.

"All right," Douglas McVea said, "everyone know what they have to do?"

Forrester nodded.

"I'm set!" Burke said quickly, his voice thick.

McVea looked at Rameri. "You?"

"Don't worry about me, McVea," Rameri said, smiling. "I've been ready all my life."

McVea studied the man for a moment. Rameri stared back unblinking. McVea looked away, stood up.

"Remember, we do no shooting unless we have to," he said. "It'd spoil the whole plan, ruin the time-table."

"Sure," Rameri said, slamming the bolt shut on the last rifle. "I'll write it on my sleeve. 'Unless we have to'!"

Again McVea stared at the massive Rameri. But Rameri said nothing more, just sat and lightly stroked his weapon.

"Okay," McVea said. "It should be a great game to-night. We wouldn't want to miss it, would we? Let's go!"

9

Outside the Sports Arena the last-minute arrivals didn't even glance at the four men transferring cameras and equipment cases from a closed van to a pair of dollies. The fans hurried on into the arena, where the big game between the arch-rival Bisons and Owls was already in full swing.

Packed shoulder to shoulder in the stands, the hoop devotees watched the two well-matched teams swiftly and skillfully moving the ball from end to end of the bright court, from basket to basket. The heavy pounding of feet on boards, the heavy breathing of men running at full endurance, the hard slam of the ball on the floor, against hands, off the backboards, the shouts of encouragement all rose up from the court, which was a bright pit at the center of the darkened stands.

The vast crowd yelled and cheered, rising to its feet almost in unison at every spectacular play. There were fifteen thousand people jammed side by side in the towering stands.

Up in the broadcasting booth, the Owls' long-time play-by-play sportscaster, Andy Whitaker, was flanked by technicians and a TV camera. The well-known voice was in high gear.

". . . And what a night little Ollie Wyatt is having, Owl fans! I've never seen the great All-American from Kansas State have a better one! Behind him, the Owls are pulling away, playing the way only *they* can, in almost post-season form, and—"

Hondo Harrelson leaned forward in the easy chair in his living room, his sharp eyes watching every move on the basketball court on his TV screen. Andy Whitaker's voice rose high.

". . . Now the Bisons move into a full-court press! They're trying to stop the Owls' momentum. The Owls work the ball up court. The Bisons steal it! A fast break. . . . Oh, little Ollie Wyatt intercepts, steals the ball back, the Owls—a signal from the bench and the Owls call a time out! Folks, this—"

The doorbell sounded through Hondo's house. He got up, his eyes turned back toward the TV set, and opened his door. Deacon Kay came in carrying a large, flat box—a pizza.

"Deke, what—?" Hondo began.

"I got an urgent message," Deke grinned. "From our good wives at the P.T.A. meeting—get some food over to Hondo before he starves to death. So, *voilà*, food!"

Deke opened the box with a flourish, displaying the pizza. Hondo didn't look at it. His eyes were glued on the TV screen.

"Hope you don't mind," Deke went on. "One lovely pizza with mushrooms and sausage."

Hondo turned. "What? You know I hate mushrooms and sausage."

"Gee, must have slipped my mind," Deke beamed. "I love mushrooms and sausage."

"Why, you ornery—"

Deke laughed and held the pizza out. "Relax, it's got anchovies all over it—the way we *both* like it!"

Hondo shook his head, and they each took a slice, settling in front of the TV set.

"How're we doing?" Deke asked, taking a huge bite.

Hondo chewed hungrily. "Forty-eight, fifty-three Owls. Ollie's already got seventeen points."

"Boy, how can anyone that small make it in the pros?"

"He says his wife told everyone he was seven-foot-one." Hondo grinned.

"Man," Deke said, "he sure plays like it."

Both men leaned forward, watching intently as Ollie Wyatt brought the ball slowly up court, directing his taller teammates.

In the arena, the crowd leaped up as Ollie suddenly flashed in at a sharp angle, swept past the Bison defense, and leaped high to deftly lay one in. The arena roared as Ollie hustled back on defense, smiling and back-pedaling, all the time keeping his eyes fixed on the ball in the Bison guard's hands.

On the sidelines, Douglas McVea stood beside Rameri's movie camera.

"Did you see that?" McVea said. "He's some player—a million-dollar star!"

"Two million," Rameri said, working his camera.

Behind them, carrying equipment boxes, Burke and Forrester also watched the action on the court. Burke seemed involved, excited. Forrester looked at the younger man in disgust, his own cold eyes roaming across the packed stands, studying the exits and uniformed guards.

"The guards are pretty relaxed," Forrester said.

"Why not?" McVea said. "What can happen here?"

Rameri said, "Only a couple of seconds to half time. Is everyone ready?"

Burke swallowed hard. "Yeh, sure."

"Bombs away," Forrester said, and he patted the camera case he was carrying.

"Remember," McVea said, "we just walk into the locker room bold and straight. Don't act nervous.

Our setup in the locker room's been okayed—all part of the documentary."

"Yeh," Rameri said with his thin smile, "the best part."

As his words faded, a Bison player sank a last-second basket out on the court, and the half-time buzzer sounded through the arena. The teams trotted off toward their respective locker rooms.

On the sidelines, the documentary crew began to push their equipment in the same direction.

"Just walk easy," Douglas McVea said. "Take a nice, slow setting-up inside. Nobody's even going to see us."

On his fourth slice of pizza and his second beer, Hondo Harrelson beamed at the TV set—the Owls were winning.

". . . What a first half, folks!" the voice of Andy Whitaker said. "Ollie Wyatt hasn't been this hot since the Owls swept through the playoffs last year. I don't know what they're feeding the little man, or maybe it's the beautiful Joanne Wyatt and the little hoopster she's about to present to Ollie, but—"

Hondo stood to turn down the sound, gesturing toward Deke Kay's empty beer can.

"Want another beer, Deke?"

"Can a fish swim?" Deke grinned.

Hondo blinked at the set and spoke again without turning. "When will the girls be home?"

"After the game," Deke said. "I hope."

"Yeh," Hondo said, but his voice was distant, and he went on staring at the now silent TV set. "Deke? I thought Pete Morgan, the Owls' coach, had a strict rule of no one being allowed in the locker room between halves?"

"He does. Made a big announcement about it just

last week again," Deke said. "Said he wanted everyone to know so no one would feel offended."

"Yeh," Hondo said. "Look at those guys, Deke."

Deke Kay looked at the set. Four men were pushing dollies loaded with cameras and cables down the locker-room entrance ramp. He frowned.

"It must be that documentary crew T. J. told us about," he said. "Maybe there's something else down that ramp besides the locker rooms."

"What?" Hondo said. "I've been down there."

"You think they're up to something?"

"I don't know," Hondo said, "but I'm going to find out."

He strode to his telephone. "Harrelson here, Olympic S.W.A.T. Get me Chief Roman, urgent."

Deke Kay went on scowling at the screen. The four men of the documentary crew had now vanished down the ramp to the team locker rooms.

10

In the Owls' locker room under the stands, trainer Bill Grainger stood back as Ollie Wyatt led the players in. They were shouting and slapping each other on the rump as they piled through the door, leaving a crowd of reporters and jubilant fans out in the jammed corridor. Grainger tossed them all warmup jackets as they spread through the room to sit on the benches and go over the triumphs of the first half.

"Ollie, man, you ain't never played taller!" big Sandy

Agee shouted. The six-ten center pounded Ollie Wyatt on the back.

"Did you see me leave old Slats Kelly nailed down on that sneaky fall-away?" shouted Don Benson, the backcourt man.

"Kelly been looking the wrong way all night!" shouted back Turk Jensen, the six-six forward from Cal State Long Beach.

"Hey, don't get too cocky, guys," Ollie warned. "Dutch'll send those Bisons out eating raw meat after the half, and if we let down we'll be the meat."

"Ah, they won't even get an appetizer out of us tonight," said Solly Beckberg, the seven-foot backup center.

"After that session, they ain't got no teeth left to eat nothing but our dust!" Cal "The Bull" Vasquez cried.

Bill Grainger listened to the exuberant players with a small smile. The trainer was always pleased to see his charges fired up, but he also knew the dangers of overconfidence, and he approved of Ollie Wyatt's quiet leadership of his teammates. He was watching Ollie to see if the All-Pro's next move would calm his red-hot mates, and only glanced at the door when it opened again.

For a moment Grainger frowned as he saw the four strangers enter carrying hand-held cameras, loops of cable, recorders, and heavy cases. Then he nodded, recognizing the documentary film crew Robin Phillips had spoken of, and looked back toward Ollie Wyatt. The guard was leaning calmly against a locker.

"Sure, Cal, we'll give 'em plenty of dust to eat," Ollie said, "only let's be sure we don't get to laughing so hard at them that they run right through our dust to the bucket."

"Aw, Ollie, they ain't got a hope tonight," Don Benson said.

"Even I'm beating Kelly off the boards tonight," Solly Beckberg cried.

"Sure," Sandy Agee agreed. "I think I'll take the night off the rest of the way, let Solly build his average."

They all laughed, none of them really noticing the four men placing equipment boxes against the walls, taking light readings, setting volume and tone dials on the recorders. Unobtrusively the four film-makers spread through the room, never moving more than a step or two away from their equipment and cases.

"Right," Ollie said. "Sandy, you take the rest of the game off. Solly, you try to go the rest of the way against old Slats Kelly. Cal, you laugh all the way out there. Go on, all of you—that's just exactly what Dutch Kale wants. Go on, give him a good night—you know how Dutch likes to beat the Owls. Keep it up, and make Dutch the happiest coach in the league!"

The players looked at each other, slowly coming down from their first-half high. Don Benson shrugged. Big Sandy Agee began to nod.

"Right on, Ollie," Douglas McVea said, standing beside Rameri, who held a camera. "You tell them. And hold that pose a minute, okay?"

Ollie glanced toward the smiling McVea and nodded. He remained leaning against the locker. The other players stood self-consciously as Rameri worked his hand camera. A few of them looked at each other as if they were wondering what the cameramen were doing in the locker room. Ollie shrugged.

"One of Miss Phillips' brainstorms," he said. "A documentary. We're all going to get immortalized—and sell a lot of extra seats."

Rameri finished shooting and moved across to the far side of the locker room. Forrester was close to one side wall, Burke near the other. McVea was just inside the door.

"Okay, now just go on about what you usually do," McVea said.

Don Benson said, "I usually strip and cool off."

"Okay," McVea said, laughing. "This is a documentary—we want it all real. Maybe you'll sell a lot of tickets to the ladies, Benson."

Sandy Agee said, "God, they'd run screaming."

"Or die laughing!" Solly Beckberg yelled.

"Maybe cry a lot!" Cal Vasquez shouted.

The others took up the kidding—and then Pete Morgan, the famous Owls coach, walked in. From his eyes, you could see that Morgan was pleased with his players, but the rest of his craggy face didn't show it. He looked grim and serious, and he held a notebook full of notes.

"All right, you clowns, simmer down!" the coach said, his voice brusque. He glared at his men as they made him the center of attention. He waved the notebook. "Now I've got a couple of little notes for you all."

The locker room erupted in a chorus of groans as the players formed a ring around their coach. Each player was anxious to know if his name was in the notebook.

Unobserved, McVea motioned Burke toward the door into the corridor. Silently Forrester eased up against the wall at the rear, next to the door into the showers. Rameri carefully put his camera on a bench and slowly lit a cigarette, his small, hard eyes watching every movement in the room.

"Okay," Pete Morgan snapped. "You, Turk, now what the hell were you doing when Ollie passed—" He suddenly stopped, his attention caught by McVea, who was aiming his camera at him. His face turned beet red. "You! Over there! The joker with the camera! What the hell do you think you're doing?"

Startled by the sudden attention, McVea almost

63

dropped his camera. He smiled at Pete Morgan and started to speak, but Morgan cut him off. "Half-time meetings are closed to the press, you hear? Closed to everyone!"

"We're not the press, Coach," McVea said evenly, his composure recovered. "We're filming a documentary on the team. Miss Phillips gave us—"

"I don't care if you're filming *Airport '77*." Morgan roared, motioning to trainer Bill Grainger. "Get them the hell out of here! Now!"

The trainer moved toward McVea. As he did, Rameri bent down and opened the lid of an equipment case at his feet. McVea smiled and looked at Pete Morgan.

"No, we won't get out. As a matter of fact, Coach," and McVea nodded toward Rameri, "no one's going anywhere!"

Rameri came up from his equipment case with the lethal automatic rifle aimed straight at Pete Morgan.

"Nowhere at all," McVea said, still smiling.

Rameri held the deadly gun, his small eyes glittering. He licked his lips as he slowly moved the rifle in a sweep of the silent locker room.

Lieutenant Hondo Harrelson waited with the telephone in his hand. Deacon Kay watched him in the flickering light of the silent TV set.

"Chief?" Hondo said quickly. "I'm watching the Owls game on TV. You happen to see the half time?"

Chief Roman's voice was testy. "I've got better things to do than watch some damned game, Hondo. If that's all—"

"Hold it, Chief," Hondo cut him short. "Maybe it's nothing, or maybe it's something big. You know Pete Morgan never allows anyone in the lockers at half time? Not even the team's owner?"

"Everyone knows that, damn it," Chief Roman said. "I—"

"Well, we just saw a documentary camera crew go down toward the locker rooms," Hondo said. "T. J. talked to that crew today, said there was something funny about them. Can you check it out, get someone to find out who they are, where they come from?"

Roman was silent a moment. "Okay, Hondo, I'll have it checked. Stay at your phone."

The chief hung up. So did Hondo, and he stood thinking for a moment. Then he picked up the phone again.

"Street?" he snapped into the instrument. "Get T. J. and Luca on the alert—everyone get ready to move and stand by."

He hung up again, looked at Deke. The big man was watching the silent TV screen.

"It all looks quiet, Hondo," Deke said.

Hondo joined him, and both men stared at the intermission scene in the crowded arena. Nothing unusual seemed to be going on; the crowd were milling and eating and enjoying themselves.

"I hope to hell it stays that way," Hondo said. "I hope I'm all wrong."

They both went on staring at the screen.

In the shocked locker room, McVea took another automatic rifle from an equipment case. At the door, Burke held his automatic weapon in one hand and reached behind him with the other to lock the door into the corridor. Forrester stood behind the team gathered around Morgan, aiming his rifle.

"The man said it," Forrester said. "No one goes anywhere, not even to take a shower."

The startled athletes turned, milled around, and stared in unbelieving bewilderment at the four rifles aimed at them. It was Ollie Wyatt who found his voice first.

"Hey, what is this? What's going on?"

"You'll find out, little man," Rameri said.

Solly Beckberg's eyes snapped. The giant backup center took a step forward. "You punks better—"

McVea swung his rifle menacingly. "No heroics, gentlemen, please. If everyone will stay cool, no one will get hurt."

Pete Morgan stared at McVea, looked at all four guns one at a time. The coach's eyes were incredulous.

"You've got to be kidding," Morgan said. "We've got a second half to play in five minutes! Now you get out—"

"Shut up!" McVea snapped. "The Organization for the Freedom of Oppressed Peoples doesn't kid, Mr. Morgan! We want to—"

Half hidden behind two of his taller teammates at the far end of the locker room, Don Benson, Ollie Wyatt's backcourt partner on the starting Owls team, watched the four terrorists. A feisty firecracker, Benson was known for having a short fuse that got him into trouble. Now his snapping eyes seemed to smoulder, and it was obvious that he was fed up to his eyeballs with whatever the four gunmen thought they were doing.

"Hey, man," Ollie began, "we're just hardworking boys who—"

Suddenly Don Benson pushed past his taller buddies, moving toward McVea.

"Aw, let's cut this crap! You take those cannons and—"

The four rifles swung toward Benson. Ollie Wyatt tried to intervene. "Baby, cool down! You—"

It was Rameri's rifle that spoke next in the tense locker room.

A single shot, squeezed carefully and coldly,

66

slammed into Don Benson's shoulder, spun him back-ward crashing against the lockers and bouncing off them to the floor.

Solly Beckberg jumped. "You dirty bastard son-of-a—"

"Solly, hold—" Ollie tried to stop the giant center. Rameri's rifle ripped a burst this time.

Solly Beckberg was almost cut in half before he pitched to the floor. Rameri smiled coldly.

"Now, why'd you all make me do that? I mean, I had to shoot, you know?" the massive gunman said. He looked all around. "Okay? Everyone convinced now?"

11

McVea stared in fury at Rameri for an instant. Young Burke was pale as a ghost, his boyish face as scared as the faces of the Owl team members. Forrester showed nothing; his face was without expression, only a faint twitch at the corner of his mouth hinting that he hadn't figured on shooting. McVea recovered quickly and faced Coach Morgan and the Owl team.

"I'm sorry we had to do that," he said calmly, "but we're soldiers in a war, and now you know we mean business. If you do what your told, no more heroics, no one else will get hurt. You all understand that?"

He looked more at Rameri than at the Owls. The squat killer went on smiling, saying nothing, enjoying the whole scene. McVea turned to Bill Grainger.

"You the trainer?" he said.

Grainger nodded.

"All right," McVea said. "See what you can do about keeping those two alive."

Grainger moved quickly to the two fallen players. Sandy Agee was bending over Solly Beckberg. He looked up at Grainger, then at Rameri and McVea.

"You can't do nothin' for Solly," Agee said. "No one can. He's dead."

An angry murmur ran through the locker room. Forrester and Rameri swept their weapons in menacing arcs, covering all the Owl players. Rameri's eyes were strangely bright, glowing. He licked lightly at his thick lips.

"Too bad," he said softly, almost in a purr. "Too bad."

Ollie Wyatt was kneeling beside Don Benson. He looked up. "Don's still breathing, but he's bleeding bad. Looks in shock."

Grainger hurried to Benson, knelt down to examine the wounded man. He got up and went to get his equipment bag. When he returned with it and began to work on the unconscious Benson, Ollie Wyatt stood up.

"All right," the Owl star said, "so you're big-time guerrillas. What the hell do you want with us?"

"First," McVea said, "we want you all to stay nice and calm. As I said, that way no one else gets hurt, and we get our business done neat and easy. So—"

Staring at McVea, Ollie said, "You're sure you *can* promise no one else gets hurt if we cooperate, mister? You're sure we don't have as good a chance to survive by jumping you?"

"You have my word—" McVea began.

"*Your* word?" Ollie said, and he looked at Rameri. "You're sure *you* can promise us anything? You're sure that gorilla isn't the boss of your gang?"

"I'm in charge of our unit!" McVea snapped. "You better believe it! Now, how do I get the broadcasting booth on the telephone?"

Pete Morgan said, "It's extension 273."

"Fine." McVea nodded. "That's the kind of co-operation we like. Now everyone hang loose and this'll all be over real soon."

McVea stepped to the wall telephone and began to dial.

In the TV booth hanging just below the upper deck of the Sports Arena, the broadcast had been switched back to the studio for the half-time sports update and spot news. Andy Whitaker was relaxing with Robin Phillips over beer and sandwiches. Whitaker was looking pleased.

"Damned nice first half," he said to the tall red-headed P.R. woman. "They play like that the rest of the season, we'll breeze into the playoffs."

"And we'll sell a lot of seats down the whole stretch," Robin Phillips said. "Unless they play too well, get too far out in front."

"You want them to play just well enough to hold about a two-game lead all the way?" Whitaker grinned. "I like a good, sharp, calculating broad, Robin."

"The name of the game I'm in." She laughed.

Robin Phillips had changed into a high-waisted black slacks suit that showed off her body well. Her smooth, tanned face looked pleased. She was sure that she was doing her job well, sure that she was working for a winner.

"You've done a great job for the Owls," Whitaker said. "I mean it."

"I try," Robin said.

"How about doing a job with me? I mean, how

about we have a little private session together?"
Whitaker said.

"Who knows?" Robin smiled. "Only wouldn't your
wife object?"

"I hope she would," Whitaker said, "but why worry
her?"

"I'll think about it after the season."

Whitaker sighed, "That's what they always say.
I—"

The telephone in the booth suddenly jangled.
Whitaker reached for the receiver.

"Yeh, Whitaker."

He listened, handed the phone to Robin. "It's for
you."

"Hello, Miss Phillips speaking," the P.R. woman
said, her voice crisp.

"Doug McVea here, Miss Phillips," McVea's
smooth voice said from the other end. "Oh, I'm sorry,
it's Robin, isn't it?"

"Robin it is," the girl said. "Is something wrong?
Everyone's cooperating, I hope."

"Everyone is being very cooperative," McVea said.
"At least they are now. I am afraid we had to do a
little unscheduled shooting, but all is very nice now."

"Very good," Robin said. "Then what's up?"

"Well, we're down here in the locker room doing
our, ah, shooting. The whole team is here, of course,
as is your fine coach Mr. Morgan. I'll put Mr. Morgan on in a moment. But first I thought I should advise
you of a few new developments. A small change in
our script, you might say."

"A change?" Robin snapped. "Now, McVea, I
approved your planned script as it was. Any changes
need authorization—"

"I'm afraid, Robin, that this change doesn't come
within your scope of authorization. In fact, its only
authorization comes from our, ah, 'parent' organization

70

—The Organization for the Freedom of Oppressed Peoples."

"What?" Robin sat up rigid. "What are you talking about? I never gave any permission to—"

"I'm talking about war, my dear Robin," McVea's voice said sharply. "Real war. The war of all the oppressed people everywhere against the imperialist nations—against your nation!"

"War?" Robin stared at the receiver. "Is this some joke? McVea, if you—"

"That's enough, Robin," McVea snapped. "We are guerrillas—terrorists, some say. We're not kidding, it's no joke, and we mean business. We are armed, we have bombs planted throughout the arena, and we are holding the whole Owl team hostage down here. Do you have that clear?"

Robis stared at the phone in stunned horror.

"I'm sure you do, don't you?" McVea went on calmly. "Now here is what we want. Meet our terms or the entire Owl team will never play another game!"

Robin Phillips began to shake. Andy Whitaker stared at her and picked up the second extension to listen.

In the Harrelson living room, Hondo and Deke were still standing in front of the TV set. The sound was back on now, and the half-time sports report and news had just ended. The arena floor was on the screen again; the preparations for the second half were almost completed.

"Where's Whitaker?" Deke said suddenly. "He should be back on by now with the second-half intro."

"Yeh," Hondo said, watching the screen. He looked at his watch. "The team's late."

"The Bisons are coming out." Deke pointed.

"But not the Owls," Hondo said.

He crossed to the telephone again, dialed. "Chief

Roman," he said. "Harrelson again. Yes, put him on."

There was a pause while Hondo fidgeted and looked back at the screen where the Owls still hadn't appeared. The chief's voice brought Hondo's attention back to the telephone.

"Harrelson!"

Hondo turned to the phone, "Yes, Chief. You checked those film-makers out?"

"I started to, but now we don't have to. They've just checked themselves out!"

Hondo gripped the phone hard. "How, Chief?"

"They contacted the Owls public-relations people at the arena. They're the terrorist gang, all right, and they're holding the entire Owl team hostage! They've threatened to kill them all unless we meet their demands."

Hondo stood there holding the receiver for a long minute. So there it was. It had happened in his territory at last. . . .

"Goddamnit," Captain Dawson had said back then in Los Angeles, "why did it have to happen in my beat? How do you handle it, Harrelson? How?"

"What demands, Chief?" Hondo said.

"Reassessment of our Middle East policy, and no more arms to Israel. Immediate release and safe-conduct for members of their group in American jails—including that Nicholas Cortease you've got. Two million dollars in cash, and—"

"Safe transportation to the airport, a jet waiting with a full crew and full tanks," Hondo finished. "It's standard."

"It's also impossible. I'm in touch with City Hall, Sacramento and Washington, but right now it's our baby," the chief said. His voice was tight, tense. "Our baby—an arena full of fifteen thousand innocent bystanders, the whole Owl basketball team, a thousand arena employees, and the night-club district all around full of tourists. They've got automatic rifles, and they've planted bombs."

"Okay," Hondo said, "our baby."

The chief was silent a moment. "It's what you've been training for. What we both know S.W.A.T. was created for. It's *your* baby, Hondo. Take over."

"Will do," Hondo said. "We're on our way."

He hung up and just stood there for a time. Across the room, Deke Kay watched him. Hondo took a deep breath, looked toward Deke.

"They've hit us. They're holding the whole Owl team for ransom."

"The whole—" Deke looked toward the screen. The Bisons were still warming up for the second half. "But that's impossible! We're watching the game right there!"

Hondo looked at the screen. "We're not watching the Owls. The terrorists are down in the locker room —that documentary film crew. They've got guns, bombs, and they've threatened to kill the entire team if we don't meet their terms."

He picked up the telephone again and dialed the S.W.A.T. war room. Jim Street answered at once. "We just heard from the Communications Center, Lieutenant! We're all ready to roll!"

"Check," Hondo said. "Deke and I'll roll from here. If you arrive first, set up a command post and wait for us. But don't block the main entrance—they'll probably try to clear out the arena if the terrorists let them, and the fans'll be packing the exit."

"Ten-four," Street said, and hung up.

Hondo started for the door. "We'll change as we roll, Deke. Let's hope those terrorists know what the hell they're doing."

Deke followed Hondo out. "You want them to be good at this? Why?"

"I want them to be perfect," Hondo said grimly. "One mistake, and we could lose the whole Owl team, not to mention fifteen thousand spectators and a couple of thousand tourists in the night clubs around the arena!"

"What do we lose if they *don't* make any mistakes?" Deke said as they reached Hondo's car.

"Just two million dollars," Hondo said. "That's all, just two million dollars."

12

In his speeding car, red toplight flashing through the city night, Hondo spoke curtly into the radio. "Communications Center! Try to get the Owl management to clear the arena! Street! When you arrive, seal off the front exit—no one out except unarmed fans. The chief has Sunset and Riverside S.W.A.T. on the way too. They'll seal off the sides and rear."

The Olympic S.W.A.T. van hurtled down the city street. Street bent to the radio.

"Got it, Hondo. E.T.A. five minutes."

T. J. leaned over his shoulder. "Sir! We got word some players have been shot, maybe some are dead! Ollie Wyatt's down in that locker room!"

Dom Luca said, "Take it easy, T. J."

"Who's gonna tell Joanne?" T. J. said. "Someone oughta tell her before she gets it on TV!"

74

In the broadcasting booth of the Sports Arena, Andy Whitaker mopped sweat from his face and talked hoarsely into the mike.

". . . This is Andy Whitaker repeating that the Owl management has announced that due to circumstances beyond its control the game will not be completed tonight. All tickets will be honored at the next home game. Please leave quietly. I repeat again, the game cannot be completed tonight. Please leave by the main entrance and keep your tickets."

Whitaker sat back, wiping his pale face. He looked at Robin Phillips.

"I hope to hell they get out fast!"

Robin said nothing.

Hondo swung the wheel savagely and sent the speeding car down a long avenue. Startled motorists wildly pulled out of its way.

"Van, come in!" he snapped.

He had gotten into his dark blue S.W.A.T. battle uniform and flak jacket while Deke drove, and now Deke was putting on his attack clothes and checking out the weapons.

"Riverside and Sunset S.W.A.T. teams, establish a perimeter," Hondo went on, "and come in, van!"

Deke slammed a loaded clip into Hondo's carbine.

"Ready," Deke said.

The Olympic S.W.A.T. van was parked at the front entrance to the arena. The disgruntled fans were slowly filing out, complaining loudly. In the back of the van, Luca and T. J. were checking out their weapons, ordering the attack and communications gear. Jim Street was at the radio.

"The arena's still being emptied, Lieutenant," Street

reported. "No terrorists in sight, no bomb explosions, no sign of any Owl players. Street police are keeping the crowd moving, have the front sealed off. They're keeping the loading entrance clear for us."

Deke Kay had the wheel of Hondo's car again. Hondo sat beside him, his carbine in one hand, the radio mike in the other.

"I want every damned detail of what's happened, where everyone is! All the particulars, Street! Who's in charge down there for the Owl management?"

In the van, Street put down his radiophone. "The club owner's out of town, Lieutenant. He's been notified of the action by the club's P.R. exec. A woman, name's—" Street glanced at a pad of notes on the small van desk in front of him—"Robin Phillips. She's acting on the owner's orders, with full authority, until he arrives."

In his car, Hondo hung on as Deke turned a corner on two wheels, sending a Buick almost up onto the sidewalk. When the car got back on an even keel, Hondo bent to the microphone again.

"Okay. Get this Miss Phillips where we can talk with her. I want her available the moment we arrive —with a floor plan of the whole arena inside and out!"

From the van at the arena, Street's voice acknowledged. "Got it, Lieutenant."

Hondo flicked a dial. "Communications Center! Send the bomb squad to the Sports Arena; as soon as the last of the audience is out, they're to make a complete sweep of the entire place. I want them to tear the place apart if they have to, but they're to find any bombs—and fast!"

Working in the rear of the S.W.A.T. van with its complete control and tactical-equipment center, Jim Street broke his connection to Hondo Harrelson in the car, turned some dials on the radio console, pulled some levers, and bent to the mike again.

"P.C., this is Olympic S.W.A.T. field control. Patch me into the Sports Arena telephone lines. Red alert priority."

Street waited, drumming his fingers on the console. Dom Luca, completing his final weapons check in the back of the S.W.A.T. van, shook his head.

"These terrorists must have really gone nuts, flipped out all the way."

"What makes you so sure?" T. J. asked.

"Tell us all about it," Street said, grim. "You've got some inside dope, Luca?"

"Sure," Luca said. "I mean, you think they would have tried this caper if they knew what kind of an Owl fan old Hondo Harrelson is? Man, he'll tear 'em apart and eat 'em up!"

Jim Street smiled. T. J. didn't.

"I don't think it's all so funny," T. J. said.

"Hey, come on," Luca said. "Let's not get uptight, Dudley Do-Right."

"I was just thinking about Ollie," T. J. said. "Ollie's in there, Luca, and to me it just isn't very funny."

The peppery little Italian turned red, his happy-go-lucky eyes clouding. "Hey, T. J., I'm sorry," he said.

The radio console droned. "You're now tied in with the Sports Arena, Olympic S.W.A.T. field control. Go ahead."

The trio in the van instantly forgot their personal affairs; Street bent to the mike. "This is Officer James Street, Olympic S.W.A.T. field control. Connect me with Miss Robin Phillips, urgent!"

77

High in the broadcasting booth, Andy Whitaker watched the floor below as the last of the reluctant fans, with a final angry heave of programs and beer cans, trickled out down the main exit ramp. He leaned back in his chair, almost collapsing, and turned to Robin Phillips. "Well, at least they're safe. No bombs."

"No," Robin said, her face pale and drawn by the strain. "Not yet, thank God!"

"Now we just have the team to worry about," Whitaker said in the voice of a man saying that the rain had stopped, now all they had to worry about was the flood.

"What can we do?" Robin said, her voice shaking. "They've got them all! We have to meet their demands."

"I guess that's up to the police, the government," Whitaker said. "I've heard the State Department and the FBI are on the way. Maybe the CIA, too."

The jangling of the telephone made them both jump a foot. They looked at the ringing instrument as if it were some deadly animal, perhaps a coiled snake. Robin finally picked it up.

"Robin Phillips."

"Miss Phillips? Officer James Street, Police Department Olympic S.W.A.T. Our lieutenant will be there any minute. He'd like you to meet him down on the arena door with full details of everything you know about this, and a blueprint of the whole arena."

"Yes," Robin said eagerly, "all right. I'll be there!"

At that moment, Hondo Harrelson's car sped down the ramp from the loading entrance and came to a screeching halt on the arena floor. Behind it, the S.W.A.T. van rolled down the ramp into the arena. Out of his car, Hondo motioned the van on into the center of the court, and he and Deke hurried after it on foot.

Behind the S.W.A.T. vehicles came some patrol cars. They spread right and left, uniformed patrolmen jumping out and hurrying to cover every exit, every aisle, every corridor in the maze under the stands.

The Sports Arena was sealed tight.

13

The S.W.A.T. van's doors opened and Street, T. J., and Luca piled out. Hondo and Deacon joined them. Except for the police at every exit and vantage point, the vast arena was deserted, echoing hollowly to their footfalls.

Street reported: "Riverside and Sunset S.W.A.T. have completed establishing the perimeter around the arena outside, the black-and-white guys are covering everything inside. The P.R. woman, Robin Phillips, is on her way down to meet us here. She says there are four gunmen in the locker room holding fourteen hostages, and some have been shot. We don't know how many, who they are, or what their condition is. We don't have an exact count on their weapons, but word says it's at least four automatic rifles and some bombs planted around the arena."

"Four bombs," a voice said.

They turned to see the uniformed captain in charge of the bomb squad. His brow was beaded with sweat under graying hair. In the distance behind him, four of his squad, wearing heavy padded jackets, face visors,

79

and steel helmets, were gingerly loading heavy metal boxes into an armored container on the back of a van.

"That's all of them?" Hondo asked.

"All we found, and we've given the place the vacuum treatment. They're disarmed and boxed, and I'll stake my reputation that we've got them all."

"Good," Hondo said. "Fast work, Captain."

"Thanks," the bomb captain said. He hesitated. "One thing, Lieutenant. They're all good bombs, expert work, nicely fused, capped, and clock-worked, but—"

"But?" Deacon said.

"They were all set to go off about two hours from now," the captain said, rubbing his grizzled chin. "That means they never really intended to blow up the audience, you know? I mean, the bombs are the work of experienced men. They had to know you'd clear the arena as fast as possible, and they didn't try to stop the audience leaving."

"That's kind of funny, isn't it?" T. J. said. "Why plant bombs if they didn't expect to blow up anyone?"

"Maybe not so strange," Hondo said thoughtfully. "The bombs were an extra negotiating point. If we didn't find them, they'd have told us when they were set to blow, used it as extra pressure to get their demands met fast so they'd give us the locations in time to disarm them. They'd especially put pressure on the arena owners to save their building. Also, the bombs would give us something to keep us busy so we'd leave them alone down in the locker room for awhile."

"It worked, too," Deacon agreed. "Except the captain there got the bombs maybe faster than they expected."

"The pressure'll work, too," Hondo said grimly.

"How?" Luca said. "We got the bombs."

"We got four bombs—we're not a hundred percent certain we've found them all," Hondo said. "They can always tell us there are more—now that we know they really planted them."

"Well, we'll keep on looking," the bomb captain said.

As he went off to send his men back to work combing the arena, he passed Robin Phillips hurrying toward the S.W.A.T. team with the arena blueprints in her hand. Her face was chalky, and her slim body in the high-waisted black pants suit seemed to be trembling.

"Lieutenant?" Her low voice wavered.

"Yes, Miss Phillips," Hondo said. "Now—"

She brushed a limp strand of thick red hair from her brow. "Robin," she said. "Please, you have to stop them!"

"We're going to try our best," Hondo said quietly.

"Yes," Robin nodded. "Yes, of course. I—" She brushed at the loose strand of hair again. "It's all my fault! They told me they were making a documentary film on the team, and I opened up all the doors for them!"

"You didn't check them out?" Hondo asked.

"I checked their references, their home office, but those were fakes, of course. Eager Robin Phillips, so anxious to prove herself, sell more tickets than anyone!"

"No one would have checked more," Hondo said quietly. "They had it well planned—probably at least one of them works legitimately for a real film company. Don't blame yourself. These are professionals —they know what they're doing."

Hondo placed a gentle hand on the slim woman's shoulder, reassuring her. With his other hand he supported her lightly as her soft body sagged against him. She seemed about to collapse. His firm touch seemed

81

to lift her, and she made an effort to pull herself together.

"They say they're from the Middle East, a Palestinian Arab group," she said. "But they don't look like Arabs—one's even black—and their names certainly aren't Arab."

Deke said, "These terrorist organizations often hire local gunmen, have non-Arab sympathizers. A lot of Japanese radicals have pulled attacks for Palestinian groups."

Hondo said, "Has there been any change in their demands?"

"No," Robin said, obviously getting her confidence back a little now that the S.W.A.T. team was here and she was doing something. "Two million in cash, a public announcement that we'll reassess our Middle East policy, release of seven of the group's members now in our prisons, a jet and crew at the airport, and the arena loading entrance to be kept open and clear."

"Okay," Hondo said. "Where are they now?"

"Still in the locker room."

"Are those the arena blueprints you have?"

Robin nodded. "Yes, a complete set."

Hondo took the rolled blueprints and began to spread them on the floor.

The Owl team sat on benches and on the floor in the heavy silence of the locker room. The tension was like an electric charge. Coach Morgan was the only team member on his feet, refusing to sit. McVea paced slowly back and forth, his eyes never leaving the silent wall telephone. Burke held his automatic rifle so tightly his arms were trembling.

Only Forrester and Rameri showed no nervousness or tension. Forrester had squatted down, his back against the wall at the shower entrance, his eyes almost sleepy but his rifle steady. Rameri leaned easily against a locker and smoked, his rifle lazily cradled in the crook of one elbow. He watched McVea with his small snake eyes.

"They're taking their time," Rameri said.

"Not even an hour yet," McVea snapped, taking a breath to relax himself. "They've got a lot to talk about, and they're probably contacting everyone from Sacramento to Washington."

"Maybe we should have let one bomb go off," Forrester said, "to sort of goose them a little."

Rameri said, "We could toss them a body or two." He looked slowly around the locker room at the Owls, enjoying their pale faces. "They could draw lots, or maybe go by scoring average—high scorer dies first, the big contract."

"Brilliant!" McVea's lip curled. "Kill them all, why not? Give the cops nothing to lose by rushing us. Make them think we're all a bunch of madmen who can't be trusted to act rational and keep a bargain! Go ahead! That way you'll make sure they'll never deal with us!"

Rameri scowled. "You don't scare 'em, they don't deal."

"You're an idiot, Rameri!" McVea snapped, his smooth voice scornful. "You don't make a deal like this by scaring them! You have to give them a solid alternative. You have to make them believe you mean business, yes, but you have to make them believe they can trust you, too! We've got to make them believe we want our demands more than we want to kill anyone! They've got to believe we'll play it straight, keep our side of the bargain!"

McVea shook his head. "If they get the idea we're crazy, psycho, killers, they'll never trust us and never deal!"

"Who you calling a psycho?" Rameri demanded, his rifle swinging toward McVea.

83

Forrester didn't move, but he covered Rameri. "Hold it easy, Rameri. We need everyone."

Rameri froze for an instant. There was a moment of suspended time when no one could be certain whether Rameri mightn't kill McVea no matter what Forrester did. Maybe he wanted McVea dead more than he wanted himself alive. . . . Then Rameri laughed and swung his rifle away.

"If we kill any more," McVea said, "they could get the idea out there that they have to rush us full force to save anyone. It's a delicate balance."

Rameri shrugged, picked at his fingernails. The rifle was cradled again. "It's your plan—for now."

"Thank you," McVea said sarcastically, and he looked at his watch. "We'll give them ten more minutes, then contact them again and tell them about Beckberg and Benson." He looked toward trainer Bill Grainger, who was still working over the wounded Don Benson. "How's he doing?"

Grainger didn't look up. "He's still alive, that's all."

"Work hard," McVea said. "He's a good reason for them to decide fast, get him a real doctor. Nice pressure."

Ollie Wyatt had been sitting silent all this time. He leaned back against a locker and watched the four terrorists. Now he fixed his sharp eyes on McVea pacing in front of the telephone.

"You guys really have to be bananas," Ollie said.

Rameri sneered, "Shut up, superstar. This ain't no lousy kid game like what they pay you for."

"My game isn't a psycho game," Ollie said.

"You heard him, Wyatt," McVea cut in. "I'd hate to see anything happen to you. I know you won't believe this, but I'm really a big Owls fan."

"Yeh?" Ollie studied McVea. "You know, I never knew they covered our games in Damascus. Or is it Cairo?"

"Both," McVea said lightly. "And you'd be surprised what we cover over there."

"You're real cool, man," Ollie said slowly, looking
around, "but I've got a funny feeling you never been
any closer to the Middle east than Vegas."

"Don't let appearances fool you," McVea said
evenly, "and don't get any mistaken ideas that might
make you think we don't mean business. You'd be
surprised how many non-Arabs have joined our cause,
fight with us and for us. Not everyone in this world
has scoring averages and bonuses in mind."

"Maybe so," Ollie agreed, nodding. "Sure, I can
buy that. Right on." He watched McVea, then looked
at Rameri. "Only I don't figure you guys got any
'cause' at all except the kind you can count. It's nowhere on this revolutionary bit of yours. Like, I don't
buy the act no way."

Rameri's snake eyes narrowed. "Good thing you
can't tell them outside about that, superstar—good
thing for you!"

"You better hope," McVea said, "that everyone
else buys it. For terrorists ready to kill and be killed
for a 'cause,' they'll come up with the two million
and a safe way out." McVea looked at the faces of
the Owl players. "And that's what we all want, right?
Because if they don't come up with the money, and
fast, we all lose—but you guys lose a lot more. Like,
you guys lose it all—the whole ball game."

Rameri said, "Superstar there, he's real smart." His
smile was all teeth, a humorless grin. "You better
just hope they ain't so smart outside."

14

Hondo Harrelson knelt down on the arena floor over the unrolled blueprints. Deke Kay knelt beside him; Robin Phillips and the rest of the S.W.A.T. team stood around them.

"We've got to know what's going on down there in the locker room before we can get an idea of how to handle it," Hondo said slowly, thoughtfully. He studied the blueprints intently.

"Is there a back door to the locker room?" Street asked.

"No," Robin said. "There's a side door, but it's right into the main locker area—there's no way you could open it unseen."

"How about windows in the shower room?" T. J. suggested.

"None," Robin said. "Vented and air-conditioned."

"Hondo," Deke said. "Chief Roman!"

The chief was striding across the now empty basketball floor, his steps echoing through the vast, deserted arena. With the chief was a pink-faced, iron-gray-haired man in his fifties. He wore an impeccable gray business suit, starched collar, a repp tie—and an anxious expression.

"How's it going, Hondo?" Chief Roman said as he came up.

Hondo stood up. "They're down in the locker room with the Owls team, we're up here. We've got their demands—and their threats. So far, that's it."

"You have a plan, Lieutenant?" The anxious-looking gray-haired man spoke in a crisp, curt voice. Clearly he was accustomed to making statements and having people listen to him.

Chief Roman said, "This is Mr. Warren Royce, Hondo, from the State Department. This is an international affair, of course, so he's been sent out to coordinate any federal involvement, and to negotiate with the terrorists if necessary."

"It's a very delicate matter, Lieutenant," Royce went on. "Explosive internationally, too. Naturally, Washington can't bend under blackmail and promise to abandon Israel, or even to reassess our Middle East policy. On the other hand, the world is watching, and we can't afford to have local police blunder ahead like storm troopers."

"We don't plan to 'blunder ahead,' Mr. Royce," Hondo said drily.

"What do you plan?" Royce asked curtly.

"At the moment, I plan to work out a plan—one that has the best chance of keeping the Owl players, innocent bystanders, my men, and the arena as safe as possible."

"Meaning that you also intend to attempt to capture these guerrillas, battle them?" Royce said.

"That's our job," Hondo said evenly.

"And mine is to consider the larger issues," Royce snapped. "You've considered negotiations? A compromise?"

"I'm considering everything," Hondo said.

"Time is important," Royce said. "I suggest you make your plans quickly, move without delay. In situations such as this, delay can be fatal."

"Haste can be more fatal," Hondo said. "The important thing is to be ready all the way when we do move."

Royce frowned. "I'm not at all sure we want a confrontation, Lieutenant."

"But we can't let them just walk out of there with the whole Owls basketball team!" Chief Roman said.

Hondo listened to Royce and the chief. He could hear the voice of Captain Dawson so long ago. . . .

"We can't let them bluff us, Harrelson, but we don't want any hostages hurt, or any bystanders." Crouched under cover across the street from the slum building, young Dan Harrelson watched the captain. Dawson couldn't make up his mind, was torn by doubt and indecision. *"The chief says no deal, the mayor says talk 'em out, the city council says they won't fight when they see our power coming at them, the National Guard commander says they're just yellow riffraff and he could come and blast 'em out for us."* Young Dan Harrelson said, *"We can handle it, sir. Just move in fast and hard!"* The captain chewed on his lip, looked across the street to the barricaded cellar and then up and down the line of his policemen crouched under cover. *"If we only knew what they're thinking in there, what they'll do. If I could be sure the hostages'll be okay, sure we know how to do it the best way."* Young Dan Harrelson sneered inside—the captain was weak, wishy-washy, maybe even scared.

Hondo said, "We'll get them, and we'll free the hostages. We won't let them walk away, and we won't let anyone get hurt except maybe some of us."

"It's a very delicate, important situation," Warren Royce said. "In my opinion, you had better hold off doing anything until the FBI and CIA people arrive."

"We'll take any help, sir," Hondo said.

"Good," Royce said. "I'll contact them both, tell them to come and take over. And I'll get further instructions from State."

"They can help, Mr. Royce, but we won't wait for them, and they won't take over," Hondo said quietly. "This is our job, we'll do it, and when is my decision."

Royce looked at him, and then at Chief Roman. The chief's face was impassive, but he gave a brief nod.

"I see," Royce said. "Very well, Lieutenant, do your job. But be sure you don't make any mistakes. I'll be back."

Warren Royce walked away. Chief Roman, looking worried and uncertain, glanced uneasily around the silent arena for a moment and then followed Royce. Hondo watched them go. So did the rest of the S.W.A.T. team.

"The chief's worried," Luca said.

"If anything goes wrong," Jim Street said, "he'll get roasted and crucified."

"Then let's make sure nothing goes wrong," Hondo said. "Let's show the chief we know how to do what we were trained to do."

He bent down again over the blueprints spread out on the floor of the basketball court.

"Robin," he said, "are there any tunnels out of here, maybe connecting with exits across the streets?"

Robin Phillips shook her head.

"What about private exits, special back corridors for the owners and execs that the public wouldn't know about?"

"No, nothing like that. Every exit and entrance and corridor is on those blueprints, and you've got police covering them all now."

Hondo frowned, pondered the blueprints. Suddenly he bent down closer, seemed to trace something with his finger.

"Deke! There's an air-conditioning vent in every room of the arena—including the Owls locker room." He looked around, getting his bearings. "It looks like there's a way to get into the ducts just off that entrance over there."

Deke followed Hondo's gaze with his eyes, looked down at the blueprint, and nodded. "Yeh, I see it."

"The duct looks like it leads right along the top of the locker room," Hondo went on. "Get into that duct, and see if you can get a look inside, see where the team is."

"Check," Deke said. He picked up his rifle and moved off at a trot toward the entrance.

"Street," Hondo said, "you stay at the van, keep all communications open."

"Right."

"Luca, you cover the main corridor up from the locker room. Keep in close touch with Street and sing out fast if anything goes on down there."

Luca nodded, cradled his shotgun, and moved closer to the main ramp. Hondo turned to Robin Phillips.

"Where's the best place to see everything in the arena?"

"Up in the broadcast booth."

"Okay, let's get up there," Hondo snapped. "T. J., you come with us."

They crossed the deserted court to the small private elevator that took them up to the broadcasting booth suspended just under the balcony. It was empty now; Andy Whitaker had been sent out of the arena after the spectators. Robin quickly gave Hondo the broadcaster's chair in front at the TV desk; she sat near him at the TV camera spot. T. J. took up a position from which he could guard the door that led outside under the stands.

The door opened. T. J. jumped alert, his sniper rifle aimed.

Joanne Wyatt came into the booth.

She stood there, bright and pretty and holding her

softly swelling belly in both slim hands. Her face was ashen under the smooth brown surface; fear was etched in every drawn line.

"They . . . they . . . just told me. I . . . It can't be true. No, it's not true!"

"Take it easy, honey," T. J. said.

She smiled. It was a ghastly smile. "It's a joke, isn't it? Some kind of stupid male joke!"

Robin went to her. "Joanne, sit down, and . . ."

"No!" Ollie Wyatt's wife shook her head. "I know it's just some prank. The team is always—"

"No, Joanne," Hondo said quietly but firmly. "I'm afraid it's no joke."

Joanne blinked at him. "Then . . . then they're really holding the team hostage? Down there in the locker room?"

T. J. nodded, looked away. Robin touched the girl.

"The *whole* team, Joanne," Robin said.

Joanne Wyatt began to nod. Yes. Yes, the whole team was being held hostage by some crazy terrorists. Everyone. Her Ollie, held down there at the point of automatic weapons. She suddenly walked straight to Hondo.

"Please," she said. "Please, Lieutenant, you've got to get them out of there! Give those . . . those crazy men what they want! Give them anything, but get Ollie out of there! Ollie and all the others!"

"We will, Joanne. We'll get them out."

"Will? Not *will* get them out—do it! Now!"

"We'll do it the best and the fastest way we can," Hondo said, "but we can't make any deals."

Robin Phillips whirled on Hondo. "Can't make any *deals?* They've already shot two men! Unless we meet their demands within the hour, they're going to start sending out a dead body every fifteen minutes! That's what they say! They mean it, Lieutenant, and you say no deals! A dead body every fifteen minutes!"

"Oh, God!" Joanne Wyatt cried. "Oh, my God!"

She collapsed in a heap on the broadcast booth floor.

15

The night was dark now, and the lawns around the Sports Arena loading entrance were deep in shadow. Listening to the noises of the city in the distance, Deacon Kay moved across the grass. He climbed the railing that ran around the base of the outer arena wall and reached the grilled opening to the ventilation shaft.

His rifle slung, Deke knelt down and examined the grille. It was securely screwed down, but not riveted. Taking an all-purpose S.W.A.T. tool from a hook on his belt, he opened to the large screwdriver blade and went to work on the screws. Moments later he lifted the grille off, exposing the long, narrow tunnel of the shaft fading away into blackness inside.

Deke studied the vanishing tunnel. It was narrow, but just about wide enough for his broad shoulders, and angled gently downward. Along it Deke could hear faint noises carrying from far inside the arena; distant fans pulled a draft of fresh air down along its hidden length.

Hooking his rifle to the special clips that would hold it flat against his back, Deke got down on his belly and vanished into the dark shaft.

Hondo sat at the broadcasting table in the booth high under the upper stands. His eyes studied every inch of the arena below. He could see Luca in position, Jim Street manning the communications at the van, and the uniformed patrolmen at every ramp and door-way.

Robin Phillips sat a few feet away in the TV camera spot. She hadn't spoken since her outburst. After T. J. had helped Joanne Wyatt to the owner's private lounge, Robin had slumped into the cameraman's chair. Now she was sitting very still, emotionally wrung out.

Hondo studied the blueprints spread out on the table in front of him, but his eyes weren't seeing the diagrams. "No deals," he had said. *No deals, you can't give in to punks*. He looked down toward where the ramp led to the locker rooms, then looked at Robin's weary profile.

No deals—and how many men might die because one man, Hondo Harrelson, said those two short words? How many might be crippled, how much destroyed? And how many might live, how much might be saved by those same two words? The decision of life and death, the right or wrong decision at any given second—and no one could make it but him. Once he had thought it so easy, so simple. Plunge ahead, decide!

. . . *Captain Dawson paced in the cover of the sunken areaway across from the barricaded slum cellar. Young Dan Harrelson watched him, the contempt in his eyes barely hidden. "The chief's sending some more men and rifles," Dawson said to his desk sergeant. "I've asked for tear gas, but I don't think our boys know how to get it into the place through that barricade." Dan Harrelson curled his lip—go in now, hard and fast, that was the way! Surprise those punks and old men, ram their revolution down their throats! "I've asked the mayor for instructions, asked if we can negotiate, make a deal. Maybe we can get the fire department, use high-pressure hoses and flush them out." Harrelson sneered—make a decision, damn it, Captain, make your decision hard and fast and stick to it! It was so simple—make a decision.*

Hondo wasn't sneering now, and it wasn't simple. The wrong decision and fourteen young men could die. Fourteen brilliant athletes, fourteen careers, fourteen families—and how many others down there in uniforms? The wrong decision and two million dollars would be lost, criminals would be set free—and maybe the fourteen lives would be lost anyway. Hondo asked forgiveness from Captain Dawson, as he had done many times over the years since that bloody day. The captain had died a brave man, but that had been the easy part. It had been the men he'd lost that would have tormented Captain Dawson, not his own death. He'd been a brave man, a good cop, but out of his depth that day, not competent enough because he hadn't been trained, prepared, for the task he faced.

Hondo bent to the mike. "Street, Luca, come up to the booth. T. J., report to the booth immediately."

He shut off the mike, looked at the silent Robin Phillips, and then activated his walkie-talkie.

"Deke? Come in. Give me your location. Give me a fix on you."

In the dark and narrow air-conditioning shaft, Deke Kay crawled on his belly. Faintly he heard Hondo's voice instructing Street and Luca to come to the broadcasting booth, T. J. to report. Then his walkie-talkie beeped, and Hondo's voice was beside him.

"Deke? Come in. Give me your location. Give me a fix on you."

Deke spoke low. "I'm in the second side duct to the left of the main shaft. If my diagram is right, there should be a grille over the ramp down to the locker room just ahead."

There was a silence, then Hondo's voice. "My blueprint reads the same. Move ahead to check it out."

Deke crawled on, moving very slowly in the ventilating duct, for it was a tight squeeze for the big man. He reached the grille in the bottom of the duct, flattened to look down through it.

"I can see a refreshment stand right below here," Deke said softly. "I've got to talk low—sound carries like crazy through these ducts."

"Okay," Hondo's voice said. "The blueprints show that stand right where the ramp to the locker rooms comes out into the corridor. You should have no more than twenty-five to thirty feet to go to be right over the locker room."

Deke looked ahead down the dark, narrow ventilating duct.

"I don't know," he said low into the walkie-talkie. "I can see something blocking the shaft maybe twenty feet ahead of me. Can't tell what it is in this light, but it looks like it's as far as I go."

"Hell!" Hondo's voice said.

Deke peered ahead, breathing hard in the dark tunnel.

High in the broadcasting booth, Hondo studied the blueprint of the ventilating system. He scowled at the lines and symbols, and then suddenly brightened.

"Deke! It's okay. What you see up ahead isn't

anything blocking the duct, it's a sharp bend! It straightens out again about five feet farther on, and then you should be right over the locker room."

Deke's voice came in a whisper. "Swell, only can I get around that bend? Maybe you should have sent Luca to do this snake act. I feel like the beef trust in here."

Hondo grinned in the booth. "You'll make it—just pretend your Mama Cass trying to get into a girdle. Suck it all in!"

"Yeh, thanks," Deke's distant voice whispered. "Okay, here goes around that bend. If I get stuck, you'll have to cut me out with a blowtorch."

"Too noisy." Hondo laughed softly. "We'll just blow you out with a vacuum cleaner." Then his voice suddenly became more serious. "Be careful, Deke. If they hear you, get any idea you're up there, you'll be trapped like a duck in a shooting gallery."

Deke's voice came back calmly. "No sweat, Dan. I'll float in here like a butterfly."

Flat on his belly inside the dark duct, his broad shoulders brushing the duct walls on both sides, Deke took a slow breath and began to crawl ahead.

The sharp bend was still some fifteen feet ahead.

Below, nothing moved in the deserted corridor, and the locker room ahead was strangely silent. Deke had the eerie feeling that he was crawling through narrow tunnels in some ancient, ruined castle where no one had lived for a thousand years, where nothing but ghosts and rats moved.

He reached the sharp bend, peered around the corner.

The duct straightened, then curved again some five feet farther on. Deke began to crawl around the corner.

Halfway, he stuck.

Deke shoved. The duct shook, and groaned, and Deke's rifle hit against the metal walls with a sharp click.

Deke froze. The sound pulsed along the duct like current along an electric wire. Had the terrorists heard?

Up in the broadcasting booth Hondo had heard. "Deke?"

There was a short silence. "Yeh, sorry, a tight fit. Was it that loud, Hondo?"

"On the walkie-talkie, but I don't think loud enough to have alerted them."

"Okay, problem number two—I'm stuck."

Behind Hondo, Street, Luca, and T. J. came into the booth together. They all heard Deke's announcement and hurried across the booth to stand behind Hondo.

"What can we do?" Street asked quickly.

"Nothing," Hondo said. "He's in the ventilating duct right outside the locker-room door." He leaned over his walkie-talkie. "Deke, can you take something off? Can you—?"

In the dark shaft, Deke took a deep breath, let it out slowly until his whole powerful body felt limp, and eased very gently but powerfully forward.

For a second he didn't move, and then his shoulders slid forward and he was around the sharp curve. He rested, spoke low: "I made it around," he said into the walkie-talkie. "Now it's straight for just about five feet, then another bend just like the last one."

Hondo's voice came quietly. "Take it slow, Deke. When you get around that bend you'll be inside the locker room."

Alone in the shaft, Deke nodded. "Roger. Here we go."

97

In the broadcasting booth even Robin Phillips came out of her despondent reverie and sat alert in the cameraman's chair. The S.W.A.T. team leaned over the walkie-talkie.

There was a silence. Then: "Okay," Deke's voice whispered. "I'm looking down into the locker room!"

16

The S.W.A.T. team and Robin Phillips looked at each other jubilantly in the broadcasting booth. Hondo spoke very low into the walkie-talkie: "Can you see them?"

Deke's whisper came: "Yeh, I can see them. I can see the whole room pretty good. Four guys, all with automatic rifles. Two Owls are down. The trainer's working over one—looks like Ollie Wyatt's backcourt partner, Don Benson."

"How's he look?" Hondo asked.

"Not good," Deke whispered.

T. J. leaned over Hondo's shoulder. "Who's the other Owl down?"

They all waited. Robin Phillips chewed an immaculate fingernail, her glance meeting T. J.'s. Was it Ollie Wyatt? Would one of them have to go to Joanne and . . . ?

"Looks like Solly Beckberg," Deke's voice said. "He's dead, Hondo."

No one spoke in the broadcasting booth, each was

deep in thought, busy considering how Solly Beckberg's death would be paid for.

"What are they all doing down there now?" Hondo said at last into the walkie-talkie.

"The Owls are just sitting all around on the floor and the benches. The four gunmen are spread around pretty good. One's a young punk, looks pretty nervous—might be a weak link, Hondo. He's holding his weapon so hard his knuckles are chalk."

"Who's the leader?"

Deke was silent a moment. "Looks like it's a good-looking guy with a kind of hard face. Slim guy, maybe thirty-five, in pretty good shape—sort of like an overage football player. He's pacing around the telephone, looks at his watch a lot, is sort of letting the others do the guarding. One of the others is a black, probably mid-thirties but looks older. Been-around-type, and has some scars to show for it. Cool cat, looks half asleep squatted down against the wall near the showers, but he'll move fast and sure when he has to."

"What about the fourth guy?"

"Yeh," Deke's distant voice whispered. "He's a different handful. Could even be the leader, or maybe wants to be. Under six feet, somewhere around thirty-five too. He's a gorilla—wide and thick. Heavy shoulders, short legs, long arms, and hands could hold two of even mine in one. A bull, Hondo, and his eyes look kind of crazy. He doesn't miss much, is watching the guy at the telephone as much as he's watching the Owls. He's number two, all right, might want to be number one."

"None of the Owls doing anything?"

"Mostly just sitting. What can they do?" Deke's soft voice said from the dark duct. "Coach Morgan's standing just the way he does in a game. The trainer's still working over Benson. Ollie Wyatt's with Benson, too."

In the locker room, Ollie Wyatt moved through the grim, silent players to where Bill Grainger hovered over Don Benson. No one except the black terrorist squatting against the rear wall even looked at him. The Owls slumped motionless, the strain showing on their tired faces, their eyes looking inside at their own thoughts, all of them facing the unknown future.

Ollie knelt down beside Bill Grainger and looked at him. The trainer shook his head, shrugged, spread his arms briefly to say that he had done all he could, there was nothing more he could do for the wounded player. Ollie turned back to Benson. The backcourt man tried to smile, but it came out a grimace of pain.

"Hey, partner, we got those Bisons spinnin' wheels," Benson said weakly.

"They're growing roots in the floor," Ollie said. "How're you doing, Don?"

"Hangin' in there, man, hangin' in," Benson said. He tried to grin again, then paled with the pain. "Just hope we don't . . . have to do . . . overtime."

"Hey, no way, slugger! Not with our lead," Ollie said.

"Yeh, no way," Benson said. He closed his eyes.

Ollie placed his hand on Benson's shoulder. A gentle hand, reassuring.

"Sleeping," Bill Grainger said. "The shock's bad, and he's lost blood. I've done everything I know, Ollie. I'm no doctor, but I know if he doesn't get one soon—" Grainger shook his head.

Ollie stood and walked through the tense locker room toward McVea, who still paced in front of the telephone. Forrester came alert, Rameri swung his rifle. Ollie ignored them, brushing past Rameri before the broad gunman could stop him. He stood in front of McVea.

"Don needs a doctor, mister," he said. "He needs one bad."

"He'll get one, too," McVea said, smiling. "Just as soon as we get our two million."

"He won't be much use to you as a dead hostage!"

"He is wounded," McVea said silkily. "He's one of our trump cards, the time element. A twist of pressure on the good government, eh? I'll bet your owner is out there now screaming that they've got to deal fast and save his second best backcourt ace. I mean, he can't win any playoffs and make a big profit with you alone, now can he?"

"Then why not shoot *me?* That'd be even better pressure," Ollie said, his face pale with fury.

Rameri said, "Don't tempt me, superstar."

"You?" Ollie snapped, looking at Rameri. "No one has to tempt you to shoot people—you do it for fun. That's how you get your kicks, isn't it? Hurting people. It makes you feel like a big man, important, instead of a half-psycho nothing!"

"Button your lip, superstar, baby!" Rameri snarled.

"I'll bet you tore the wings off birds when you were a slob of a kid. Beat up on little girls," Ollie goaded.

"Why, you—" Rameri swung his rifle.

McVea stepped between him and Ollie. "Put it down! Now, you hear me! Burke! Forrester!"

Rameri breathed heavily, not watching Ollie Wyatt at all now, but only McVea. His broad, flat face was scarlet, his little snake eyes dancing. His thick finger seemed to shake on the trigger, the corded muscles of his forearm standing out with effort—to pull the trigger, or to not pull it. For a long instant no one could have been sure what Rameri was planning to do.

McVea saw the struggle, and his nostrils went thin. With an effort he turned away from Rameri, turned his back and faced Ollie Wyatt again.

"You we want in one piece. If they thought you were wounded, needed a doctor, they might risk losing everyone else and rush us. No, you're our best ticket to two million dollars."

McVea went on, looking only at Ollie, "Two million—if we play it right, play it the way I planned it."

He spoke straight to Ollie, but he was talking to Rameri.

"Two million," Forrester echoed from across the room. "And McVea knows where to take us."

Rameri's thick face slowly regained its normal color, his finger slackened on the trigger. He turned away from McVea, walked to a corner and stood there looking at no one, his broad back rising and falling as he breathed hard, getting himself under control. McVea pointed to Ollie.

"Your buddy gets his doctor when we get our money," he said. "Then, and not before. Now you go over there, sit down, and shut up. Next time, I won't help you."

Ollie stared at him helplessly, turned, and walked back to where he'd been sitting. Bill Grainger went on working over Don Benson, but he was doing little more than stopping the bleeding and making the man as comfortable as possible.

McVea paced again near the telephone, looking at his watch.

Forrester seemed to doze.

Coach Morgan stood where he had all this time, watching each of his players like a hawk, as if he were in just another ball game and was wondering who was ready to go in.

Rameri left his corner, walked quietly to McVea.

"Don't do that again, McVea," he said.

"Someone has to stop you blowing the whole deal," McVea snapped.

"Not again," Rameri said, his small eyes fixed on McVea. "Not ever."

"You don't want two million?"

"No more orders. No telling me what to do," Rameri said, talking low and hard, and as if McVea hadn't said anything. "I want to kill someone, I'll kill. You hear me, McVea?"

"While I'm running this, you'll do what I say. You hear me?"

"Or?" Rameri said.

"What?" McVea said.

"Or what?" Rameri said. "If I don't do what you say, what'll you do? You better be ready to do something."

"We go on fighting among ourselves, no one wins."

"You better be ready to shoot, not talk."

"Damn it, keep your head!" McVea said.

"Be ready, pretty baby," Rameri said. "No more orders. And when it's over, you and me, we'll talk."

Rameri turned and walked away again.

In the silent locker room few had noticed the confrontation. Forrester had, and so had Ollie Wyatt. Ollie sat watching the two terrorists, his eyes thoughtful.

Only a few feet above the heads of the hostages and terrorists, Deke Kay had seen it too. Flat in the narrow duct, watching down through the ventilation grille, he whispered into his walkie-talkie: "They've got some trouble on the terrorist team, Hondo. The one I said was the leader is, but the gorilla doesn't like it all the way. Maybe we can use that."

"Any way to rush them? You up there, we hit the two doors, maybe when they're having an argument?" Hondo said from the broadcasting booth.

"No way," Deke whispered. "It's real close quarters

103

in there, just like a concrete bunker. Any shooting, and a lot of the hostages are going to end up dead."

"Can you drop in some tear gas?"

"Sure," Deke said, "but what good'll it do, Hondo? They've got that wounded man who couldn't get out, and it'd send the rest of them out into the corridor in a mob. We'd probably get most of the hostages killed that way."

The other members of the team around him, Hondo sat staring at the arena blueprints, deep in thought. There was no way into the locker room except through the two doors and the ventilation duct, and no way to flush them out and trap the terrorists in the long, straight concrete corridor. In the corridor the terrorists would have all the advantages—they would have the hostages to hide behind, and the police would have no cover.

"Okay," Hondo said into the walkie-talkie. "No tear gas, no rush. Stay where you are until I get back to you with a game plan."

He clicked off the walkie-talkie and went on studying the arena blueprints for some time. Street, T. J., Luca, and Robin Phillips watched him. Hondo slowly shook his head.

"There's no way we're going to get at them down in that locker room," he said. "Not without a lot of people getting hurt."

. . . *Captain Dawson watched the barricaded cellar across the dirty street as evening began to fall. Time was running out. "A lot of people are going to get hurt if we charge in over there." Dan Harrelson said, "We'll blast them out, sir." The mayor said, "No deals." The brave people who'd never faced a gun said, "You can't let them bluff you, no sir!" Captain Dawson said, "Let's move in." An hour later eight were dead, Captain Dawson one of them, and young Dan Harrel-*

son wasn't young anymore. Wounded, sick, in shock,
and horrified at the blood and death that filled the
filthy cellar, Dan Harrelson had grown up. . . . Dan
Harrelson had learned.

Hondo looked up. "So we'll make them come up here where we can take them."

17

Robin Phillips said, "How? How can you get them to come out when they're safe down there? Expose themselves?"

"What's the locker-room extension?" Hondo asked.

"One-fourteen," Robin said. "You're going to talk to them? Make a deal?"

"I'm going to talk—it's what they expect," Hondo said. He looked at his watch. "They should be getting pretty tense by now, beginning to wonder if we're going to deal at all, and wondering a lot about what we're doing. They're safe down there, but they're also blind—like wolves in a cave. If we're tense, so are they, and from what Deke saw going on between the two top dogs in the group, they're on edge."

In the windowless locker room, McVea had stopped pacing. He stood in front of the telephone looking at his watch. Across the room, Rameri leaned against a locker, his automatic rifle cradled easily, almost carelessly.

"They could be bringing up the army by now," Rameri said, his tone needling.

"I don't give a damn who they bring up," McVea

snapped irritably. "You know damn well we've got that all planned."

"Maybe they got some plans of their own up there," Rameri said. "Down here, we got no eyes. Maybe it'd be better if we was up where we could watch 'em. We got plenty of bodies for cover, to keep the cops honest."

"Don't be stupider than you have to be!" McVea said witheringly. "Down here they can't rush us, they can't ambush or get behind us, they can't pull any tricks on us. No matter how many men they have up there, only one at a time can come through that door. They've got no space or time to work in while we're down here; they couldn't hope to save the hostages."

"Maybe," Rameri said coldly, "but we gotta go up out of here sometime."

"When we do, Rameri, we'll have two million dollars and a police escort to protect *us!*"

"Yeh? So why ain't they called yet?" Rameri sneered.

"Because up there they're running circles, everybody with a different scheme for saving the day without paying us. Only there isn't any way. They'll pay."

"You're sure, bigshot? Maybe they ain't gonna even call at all. Maybe they're gonna let us sit here and sweat."

"They wouldn't dare—"

The wall telephone rang.

McVea looked triumphantly at Rameri. He took a slow, deep breath before he picked up the receiver. His voice came out cool and calm.

"Well," he said into the phone, "that was pretty close. Five more minutes, and you'd have had one dead basketball player in your laps. Now, who is this, and how fast do we get our negotiations wrapped up?"

In the broadcasting booth, Hondo said, "This is the police. I'm Lieutenant Harrelson. Who am I—?"

"Lieutenant?" McVea snapped. "I don't want to talk to any goddamned two-bit lieutenant! You get the chief, the mayor, the governor—and you get one or all of them fast! We're getting annoyed, you understand? You want to start sweeping up dead basketball players, you keep on dragging your tail! Now—"

"Killing hostages can work both ways," Hondo said evenly. "Maybe we'll decide we've got nothing to lose by blasting you down there. You need the threat, not the act."

"If we killed ten, maybe," McVea said. "But if we kill just one more, that's one you got to know didn't have to die. A kind of delicate balance, isn't it, Lieutenant? So maybe you better get on the pipe to someone with real authority who—"

"I have full authority," Hondo said curtly. "This is a S.W.A.T. operation, and I command the S.W.A.T. teams."

"I'm impressed," McVea said sarcastically. "S.W.A.T.? Yeh, I've heard of you boys—Special Weapons and Tactics, right? The cop commandos. Yeh, sure, they would send you in a war raid like this. The elite guerrilla-fighters. Only it won't do any good this time—we've got all the cards and you know it. Good, I'm glad they sent you in. You've got the training, so you know the score. It'll save a lot of wasted time. You're sure you've got the clout to deal?"

"I'm sure I have," Hondo said. "Do you? Tell me who I'm talking to."

Down in the locker room McVea smiled. Every eye was watching him now—the Owl players tense, hopeful, the terrorists eager, hungry, their cold eyes shining with anticipation.

"Don't push, Lieutenant. You don't have the situation or terrain," McVea said. "I command in our attack unit, we fight for The Organization for the Freedom of Oppressed Peoples, and that's all you need to know. My name doesn't matter. It'd be too tough for you to spell or pronounce anyway."

Hondo's voice said, "You plan to make jokes, or do you want to start really negotiating?"

"No sense of humor, Lieutenant? Too bad. I thought maybe two pros in a guerrilla war could understand each other and the situation a little better than that," McVea said. "All right, we'll stick to business, and you know damn well there's nothing to negotiate except the details of how you meet our demands. We've got the hand—you don't even have the cards to pull a decent bluff."

"You've got the cards now," Hondo said, "but sooner or later you have to throw some of them in to get your pot. That gives us an ace or two in the hole."

"You've got nothing! We get the two million bucks and safe passage out of this country, and you get your basketball team back and the arena in one piece. It's that simple."

Hondo blinked, eyes narrowing as he listened to McVea.

"That simple?" he said to McVea, his voice suddenly light and neutral. "You get the two million, and the jet out, and it's all okay?"

"You've got it!" McVea's voice said, amused. "I think you've got it."

"Yes," Hondo said, looking around the booth at Robin and his team, nodding to them to listen, "I think I've got it, all right. The two million, the jet waiting. I don't suppose you have any special destination you want us to prepare for you? No flight instructions just now?"

"We'll handle that," McVea's voice snapped.

Hondo said, "The State Department is still considering your demands about Israel and the reevaluation of our Middle East policy. I don't think they'll deal."

"You can't win 'em all," McVea said.

"It'll take some time to arrange the release of your pals in jail—if the other states'll let them out at all," Hondo said. "Cortease is the only one we hold now."

"No stalling, Lieutenant!" McVea said. "Don't try to hold up the money and the jet by making us wait for agreement on the release of our people. They're expendable; our Cause isn't. You can just forget that article of our program."

Hondo was silent for a moment. Then, "So you don't really care about your fellow terrorists? You'll let Cortease rot in prison, won't you? Did he know that?"

McVea scowled in the locker room, glancing quickly around. Both Rameri and Forrester were watching him. McVea controlled his voice and said into the phone, "All our men know the risk they take, Lieutenant. Just like your men. Our Cause is important, and the money will finance many victories, pay many soldiers."

"So why make those other demands if you never cared about them?" Hondo's voice said. "What were they supposed to be, a little window dressing?"

"Call them negotiable areas," McVea said evenly. "We want them if we can get them, but we were aware we'd have to compromise somewhere, and the money is number one on our priority list."

"The money and the getaway," Hondo said. "They're all that ever really mattered, aren't they? For the Cause."

109

"Money is the lifeblood of revolution and guerrilla warfare, just as it is of everything else," McVea said. "And time is running out, Lieutenant. No more talking. Do you have the money? Is the jet ready?"

"The money's on its way here," Hondo said. "The jet's being fueled, and we're arranging safe transport to the airport. I don't suppose you'll mind making the trip in a police van?"

"Not at all," McVea said. "I'll appreciate the irony of it as much as you."

"Have you arranged how to carry out your part of the deal? How you'll release your hostages? We'll have to be guaranteed that they'll be sure to reach us safely, that there's no way you could try to double-cross us."

"We'll work it out," McVea said. "As soon as we see the money and our safe conduct right here."

"You better work it out good," Hondo said.

"We will." McVea smiled in the locker room. "And, Lieutenant, one more small thing."

In the broadcasting booth, Hondo frowned. "What small thing?"

"You've got closed-circuit TV in the arena," McVea's voice said. "I know your S.W.A.T. tactics, and I don't want you trying any of your Green Beret tricks. So you get some of those TV cameras going and pipe the picture in here. Don't tell me it can't be done, because I've checked, and I know it's no problem at all."

"If there's time—"

"Make time!" McVea said sharply. "I want those cameras to show me that you don't have any of your sharpshooters staked out to pick us off, no camouflaged ambush to grab us after we turn over the hostages.

You try any of that, and there's going to be a lot of dead basketball players. You understand?"

Hondo glanced at the others in the booth. "Yes, I understand."

"Then get cracking," McVea said. "I'm going to watch your whole show on TV, and I better be able to give it a perfect rating. First, I want to see that the arena's all clear. Second, I want to see our getaway van out there under one of the baskets. Third, I want to see two million in cash right out where I can just about count it. So go to it, Lieutenant, and remember—you're on 'Candid Camera'!"

McVea laughed and hung up the phone.

Hondo held his phone for a moment, looking at it as if it could tell him something he wanted to know. Then he hung up slowly, lost in thought. He turned to Robin Phillips.

"You have a closed-circuit TV system?"

"Yes." Robin nodded. "It's piped all through the arena so the execs can watch the games, the audience, everything."

"They've done their homework, all right," Hondo said grimly. "Okay, they want it activated and piped into the locker room so they can be sure we haven't got them set up."

"I'll get on it right away," Robin said.

She left the booth. Hondo watched her go, glad to see that the action was pulling her together. He motioned to T. J., Street, and Luca the moment she was gone.

"The TV cameras'll make it harder to move on them—they know what they're doing," Hondo said. "We'll have to move into some positions fast right now and be careful we're not spotted. I've got Deke holding his position down in that ventilating duct, and the cameras can't spot him there. T. J., you go up into the high rafters above the scoreboard and lay very low. They won't spot you if you don't move."

T. J. nodded and left the booth.

"Luca, you go out into the loading entrance and take up a position outside the arena. When the getaway van, or money van, or both, arrives, get in under it with your magnetic holds, and stay there when it drives inside."

"Roger," Luca said. He trotted away.

"Street," Hondo finished, "you go make the rounds of every ramp, door, and aisle. Alert the patrolmen to stay in the open but be ready to close off everything."

Street started out of the booth. Chief Roman and the State Department man, Warren Royce, came in. The chief stopped Street.

"Hold everything just where it is." The chief faced Hondo. "You take no more action, understand. There's been a change in signals."

18

As McVea hung up the telephone, a murmur ran through the locker room. The players looked at each other. Some of them grinned nervously—it sounded as if they might get out of it alive. A few watched the terrorists angrily, as if they hated to think the killers would get away with it. McVea was all smiles.

"That's it. They're going to play it our way, and it won't be long now!" he said in triumph.

"Wow! Two million!" Burke cried, licking his lips.

Ollie Wyatt got up and went to kneel beside Don Benson. He touched the wounded man lightly. Benson's feverish eyes opened.

"Buzzer time," Benson whispered. "Full-court press, hey, Ollie?"

"All downhill now, Don, baby. A shoo-in," Ollie said. "We'll all be in the showers before you know it."

Forrester got up from his squatting position against the wall of the shower room. He stretched his legs, checked his automatic rifle. He wasn't smiling.

"I don't like that S.W.A.T. outfit in on this. They're dynamite," the big black man said.

"What can they do now?" McVea grinned. "Like I told the man, we've got all the cards."

"I hope so," Forrester said. "But we all better look real sharp everywhere when we move on up for the exchange."

"We'll look sharp," Burke said.

McVea said, "No sweat. We don't take a hand off our hostage friends until we've made sure everything's kosher."

He looked around at the tense players. Their faces showed the strain of the long wait in the silent room. Joseph Rameri had said nothing so far, but now he looked at the Owls, too.

"What do we do with all these jokers once we get out of here?" Rameri said.

Coach Morgan stepped forward. "Hey, you—"

"Cool it!" Forrester snapped.

Morgan stopped, looking at each of the terrorists. The Owl Players exchanged nervous glances, some getting up as they realized what Rameri had meant and what Coach Morgan had guessed. There was an angry murmur. McVea glared toward Rameri.

"You cool it, too!" he said.

Rameri shrugged. "We're going to have to do something with them."

Ollie stood up beside Benson. "You're getting your money and your safe passage out. You said that—"

"Shut up, superstar!" Rameri said, motioning with his automatic rifle.

McVea said, "If we get our money, they get sent back all in one piece. That's the deal."

"When?" Rameri said. "You let them go, that's the end of our edge right then. On top of that, we take them too far with us, they get to be a drag on us—we got to watch 'em. Out there, we're gonna have our hands full watching the cops. We got to watch fourteen ballplayers too, we got trouble. Fourteen's too many, and getting out of here we don't want enemies behind us."

"We'll work that out, Rameri," McVea said. He glanced at the grim faces of the Owl players. "You just keep doing what you're told, and you're all going to get out of this alive. I promise you that."

"Yeh," Rameri said. "Sure."

McVea whirled. "You damned stupid fool! You keep—"

One of the players called out, "Yeh, sure—the way Solly got out alive!"

"In one piece," another said angrily, "like Don there!"

"Maybe we got more chance if we jump—"

The four terrorists stood alert and braced, their eyes wary, their rifles covering the angry players.

"Hey," Burke cried nervously, "you guys sit down! You all sit down!"

McVea said, "Don't be stupid, now! Any of you!"

114

Forrester spoke low to Coach Morgan. "You better sit 'em all back down, Coach, or someone's gonna really get hurt—and real quick."

The big man nodded toward Rameri. The gunman had his finger on the trigger of his automatic rifle. He was almost in a trance, his shark smile showing all his teeth, his small eyes glistening.

"Time! You hear? Time out, you Owls!" Morgan cried. "Cool down! You can't run a fast break against guns! Everyone down!"

The tension hung like a straining wire about to break.

Then, slowly, the men began to sit down again. Ollie Wyatt made a show of sitting first, leading his teammates.

The terrorists remained braced and alert for a few more minutes; then they eased back, lowering their rifles. Forrester hunkered back down on his heels against the shower wall. McVea looked at his watch and began to pace again, thinking. Rameri was breathing hard, his eyes still overbright. Burke wiped sweat from his face, his hands shaking visibly, and looked all around the locker room. His eyes stopped at the blank screen of the closed-circuit TV.

"McVea?" Burke said. "You think that cop lieutenant heard what we wanted?"

"What?" McVea said, looking at Burke. "He heard, all right."

"He's sure taking his time about piping in the TV," Burke said, nodding at the blank screen.

McVea looked at the empty screen, looked again at his watch. Rameri came out of his trance and looked at the screen too.

"They're not going to do it," Rameri said. "Not the TV, not anything! They're playing you and your big schemes for a sucker!" His eyes glowed again.

115

"We'll have to shoot our way out of here. *My* way."

McVea turned on Rameri. He turned slowly, deliberately, his handsome face calm—almost too calm. He stepped closer to Rameri. His voice had a deadly quiet to it.

"I've had about enough of you, Rameri. From the start you've been out of step with the rest of us. You've crossed me and my plans all the way. If you didn't like my plan, why did you join up?"

Rameri's head and shoulders seemed to move forward. "I got nothing against the plan, McVea, just against how you handle it."

"It's my plan, and it's going to work just fine," McVea said. "I'm going to make you rich despite your stupidity."

"It better work, bright boy," Rameri said, his mouth thin.

"I don't much like threats," McVea said, stepping even closer. "All day you've been blowing off wind. Stop it. You got that?"

"I don't much like bright boys too big for their pants."

McVea was silent a moment. In the locker room, the Owls had sunk back into a kind of suspended lethargy. Only Coach Morgan and Ollie Wyatt were aware of the angry scene between McVea and Rameri. They, and Forrester, squatting down on his heels against the shower room wall.

McVea said, "You know, I don't think you want the plan to work. No. You don't want to be rich, Rameri, you just want to kill a lot of people. You're insane."

"Shut up!" Rameri snarled, going white.

"Your kicks—killing people. Killing important people is even better, isn't it? Yes, you're a nothing and you know it. Brainless and musclebound. Killing makes you feel big, gives you a thrill. You never did

116

care about the money, no. All you care about is killing these players, the big men!"

In two rolling steps, Rameri was on McVea, nose to nose, one giant hand on McVea's throat. The massive hand held McVea's neck like a toothpick. Rameri's arm muscles tightened as if he were about to lift McVea off the floor like a dangling hunk of dead meat.

They stood there, inches apart.

Only Ollie and Forrester saw the rest.

A long knife appeared in McVea's hand. A knife with its long, thin blade open and pressed against Rameri's belly.

Neither man spoke.

Rameri's small eyes flickered and his thick lips parted as the thin, sharp knife pressed into his ribs.

McVea's eyes were steady, fixed on the heavy gunman. His hand on the knife was steady.

Rameri smiled. He took his big hand off McVea's neck and stepped back. He looked down at the long, thin knife still in McVea's hand.

"Standoff, right?" he said.

"No," McVea said. "I win. Stay off my back from now on, you hear me?"

"Dry run, a little curtain-raiser," Rameri said. "You did good, bright boy, yeh. Only I kind of wonder how it'd go in the real thing? All the way for keeps?"

"Don't try to find out," McVea said. "You wouldn't live long enough to know the answer."

"I wonder if you got the real guts?" Rameri said. "Yeh, I wonder. You play good, but it takes a lot of gall to push that knife. Easy to hold, hard to push and finish."

"When this is over," McVea said, "then we'll both have the time to find out who can finish."

"I'll be waitin', yeh," Rameri said, showing his teeth again. "Yeh, just you and me."

"And a million dollars."

"That, too," Rameri said.

Suddenly Burke pointed. "Look!"

McVea looked. So did Rameri. The TV monitor on the closed-circuit system jumped into life. They could all see the empty stands of the arena with patrolmen stationed in the open at all the doors and aisles. The image changed, and they saw the empty rafters of the ceiling; the deserted corridors; the open doors of the loading entrance; the S.W.A.T. van parked out on the floor and silent. The various cameras went on panning around, showing no police hiding anywhere.

McVea looked toward Rameri. "See, it's going to work! They're going to play it by my rules! Our game—and two million dollars!"

He glared in victory all around the locker room.

19

In the broadcasting booth, Jim Street had watched Hondo after Chief Roman's sharp announcement that they were to do nothing, the signals had been changed. Robin Phillips returned to the booth and stopped when she saw Roman and Warren Royce with Hondo.

Harrelson nodded to Street. "You better get to

checking all the patrolmen. Have them hold position, sit tight."

Street nodded, glanced once at Chief Roman, and went out. Robin looked after him, obviously puzzled by the uneasiness in the broadcasting booth.

"I said no action, Hondo," Chief Roman said. "I mean it. It's out of our hands now."

"We can't just sit here and do nothing!" Hondo said.

"If those are the orders, that's what we do," Roman said.

Robin Phillips exploded, rage in her voice. "Do nothing? Orders? Whose orders? There are fourteen innocent men down in that locker room. They're going to kill them! You understand that? They're going to kill them! And you smug old men stand here and say you're going to do nothing!"

"No one will be killed, Miss Phillips," Chief Roman said. "That's exactly *why* I've ordered Lieutenant Harrelson to do nothing more."

"There'll be no more trouble, young lady," Warren Royce said. "I can guarantee that now."

"Guarantee?" Hondo said to Warren Royce. "You mean we fold, no more trouble for the terrorists."

Chief Roman said, "Washington thinks—"

"No!" Hondo snapped. He shook his head sharply. "You can't trust them, Chief. Once they realize we're not going to try to stop them, that they're in no more danger, they'll up their demands to the sky, and in the end they'll kill the whole team! One of them is almost a psycho, we know that now!"

"Lieutenant," Warren Royce said, "I appreciate your opinion. Chief Roman has spoken in glowing terms of you and your S.W.A.T. team. But your way isn't the only way to handle this kind of situation, and I'm sure you wouldn't presume to think that only you

119

could be right. This is a unique situation, one in which a local policeman couldn't possibly appreciate all the ramifications and considerations."

"All right, I admit that," Hondo agreed. "But I do know—"

"I'm sorry, but you don't know," Royce said. "Under the circumstances, after a full analysis of the affair, it's been decided to grant as many of the terrorists' demands as we can."

There was silence in the booth. Robin Phillips began to nod—yes, all right, anything to free the fourteen players down in the locker room. Hondo stood alone.

"That won't be hard now," he said. "All they really want is the money and a getaway. You won't even have to lose any face in the international power fight. No prisoners go free, and you stand firm on our Middle East policy. It'll look like a solid compromise."

Royce smiled. "Then it's perfect! That's exactly the right way to handle it."

"No," Hondo said, "it's exactly the *wrong* way to handle it. You can't give in to these terrorists. Not this gang. They—"

Royce cut in. "Lieutenant! I appreciate your concern—it's your job. But we have our job in Washington, and we've made a policy decision, and that's it! We all have our orders."

Hondo was silent again. Then he said, "The money's on its way? The plane is ready?"

"Yes," Royce said. "The owner of the Owls club has contacted his bank. The money and a van are already on their way. A jet capable of making the nonstop flight to the Middle East should be arriving at the airport any minute now, with a full military crew with orders to take the guerrillas wherever they want to go in the Arab world."

"If that's where they're going," Hondo said.

"What?" Royce scowled. "Where else would Arab terrorists go? What does it matter exactly where they want to be taken, anyway?"

"In this case, I think it matters a lot," Hondo said. "Mr. Royce, you notice that they haven't said yet just where they want to be flown? Or where they wanted us to fly the prisoners we have from their group? They usually announce that."

"I'm sure they have their reasons," Royce snapped.

"And I'm sure you people usually know what you're doing in these affairs. But not in this case. When you pay them their money, they'll take some of the hostages with them. That's standard—they have to keep some protection until the jet is in the air at least. If we let these terrorists get away from here with any hostages, those hostages' lives aren't going to be worth one cent."

"Lieutenant, give us some credit. We're quite aware of the fact that they'll keep at least some of the hostages with them all the way to their destination," Royce said calmly. "We have already contacted the power sources in the Arab world and have been assured that the hostages' lives will be protected the instant the plane reaches its destination."

"If it ever reaches a destination in the Arab world. If it ever reaches any destination we know. *If!*" Hondo said.

Chief Roman broke in sharply. "We're not debating here, Hondo. We've got our orders. This thing rates as an international incident, and Royce is in charge. We have to follow orders—all of us—whether we agree with them or not."

"The important thing is to get the players free and safe," Robin Phillips said. "Let those terrorists go with their loot!"

"We must avoid an international outcry at all costs," Warren Royce said.

Hondo began to pace the broadcasting booth, his face grim, fighting to keep himself under control. He waited while each of them had his say, pacing silently, his mouth a thin line. When Royce finished speaking, Hondo turned to them.

"Listen to me, all of you. I don't believe these terrorists are going to the Middle East at all. I think they're going somewhere we don't know, and somewhere they won't tell us—because they plan to run and hide, and they won't want any witnesses to say where! Once they get to wherever they're going, they'll kill the hostages they have with them and the whole jet crew!"

The others watched as he paced the booth.

"Ridiculous!" Warren Royce said. "The Organization for the Freedom of Oppressed Peoples has always kept its bargains. It is a legitimate guerrilla organization with every reason to—"

"Sure," Hondo broke in, still pacing. He stopped. "But I don't believe that those men down in the locker room are what they say they are! I don't believe they're members of The Organization for the Freedom of Oppressed Peoples at all!"

In the broadcasting booth the silence seemed to stretch out for an endless instant. It hung there, suspended, like some great black cloud.

"What do you have to base that on, Hondo?" Chief Roman said at last. "What proof is there?"

"First, none of them *are* Arabs, or even aliens, from all I can see. The sniper we caught, Cortease, is a local small-timer with a record a mile long, and he's never been out of California. I don't think he ever intended to hit the ambassador. It was almost impossible to miss from where he was—yet he missed! He lost his head, probably after hitting someone by accident, and shot up the street to make it look like he was a real terrorist who'd gone crazy with his hatred of America and Americans."

He looked around. "I think that whole attack on the ambassador was a setup to make us believe the gang consisted of real terrorists. They wanted us to *expect* a terrorist attack so we'd believe it was really a political action! The ones down there in the locker room don't give one damn about politics, or about Cortease in jail. All they want is the ransom. It's a pure extortion scheme to get money for *themselves!*"

Royce said, "That's all a wild guess, Lieutenant. Pure supposition. You have no proof, and——"

"I have enough proof for me," Hondo said, pacing again. "I *know* I'm right. I feel it in my gut. The way that leader down there talked, his evasions, his willingness to drop every demand except the money and the escape. The other demands were just window dressing, a con game to fool us."

He thought hard as he paced. "Look, that telephone call that told us about the shooting at the ambassador —it came in too soon, I see that now. The shooting on that street couldn't even have started when we got the call! It had to be one of the four down there in the locker room who called us! A setup, Chief, and they didn't plan to kill anyone on that street, but Cortease lost his head.

"Take the bombs they planted. The bomb squad said that they were all set to go off late, probably not until they were sure the arena would be clear. They wanted the bombs found in time—that was just more window dressing. Real terrorists would have kept us hanging about the bombs, made sure one went off somewhere to scare us.

"But the real key is Nicholas Cortease. He gave up! You understand? He gave up, and too easily.

Real terrorists rarely give up. They want to die when they're cornered, especially if they've failed in their mission. They can't wait to become martyrs to the Cause. Real terrorists don't abandon their political demands so easily! They don't make it such a simple matter of give them the money and a getaway and they'll vanish fast.

"No, real terrorists want the publicity, the free TV and newspaper space. They want to broadcast their Cause to the whole world. Attention is what they really want, and they make sure their Cause and demands stay right out front. They talk about their Cause and grievances. The four downstairs talk about nothing but money!"

Hondo stopped. They were all watching him now. Chief Roman was frowning with doubt. Robin Phillips looked frightened again. Warren Royce had no expression at all, the trained diplomat.

"Mr. Royce," Hondo said quietly, "I'm saying that those gunmen aren't terrorists at all. They're simple criminals, and if we let them fly off with two million and some hostages, we'll never see the hostages or the jet crew alive again."

He waited. They said nothing. Royce only watched him.

"I'm asking you to forget those orders you've got and let me and my men handle this like a straight hostage situation."

Royce hesitated. Then, "I'm sorry, I can't do—"

"You've got to do it!" Hondo insisted, his face tense. "Otherwise there're going to be a lot of innocent victims before this is over. Believe me!"

He and Warren Royce looked at each other for a long moment.

"You've got to believe me," Hondo said.

Another minute passed in the silent booth. Then

Warren Royce nodded once and walked toward the telephone.

Hondo turned quickly to Chief Roman. "Now we have to move fast. It's time to go to work and take them!"

20

Alone, Hondo walked across the basketball court to the open loading entrance. He stopped there, aware of the closed-circuit TV camera scanning his back. For a moment, nothing moved in the narrow loading area entrance.

Then the police van appeared, coming slowly up the ramp and into the loading area. Unseen, Hondo motioned to the van to stop in the entrance. He went to stand beside the driver's seat, still in full view of the camera at his back. He waved to the drivers to bring out the money, and spoke softly. "Street, are you out there?"

Jim Street's voice came low. "Yes sir, just at the gate."

"Move into that small doorway inside the entrance. Stay behind the van—the camera can't pick you up there. Get into position low in the doorway and don't move. You'll be hidden by the shadows in the doorway—as long as you don't move a hair."

"Check," Street's voice said softly.

Two armored-car guards appeared from behind the parked van, each one dragging a heavy sack. They put the sacks down in front of Hondo and handed him a receipt book. Hondo signed it, speaking low again as he wrote. "Luca? You're under the van?"

Luca's voice came almost beside him. "Yeh, I'm locked on under here good."

"All right. Stay there—don't come out. I'm going to drive the van inside the arena. Be ready for anything."

Hondo finished signing the receipt book, handed it back to one of the armored-car guards. They moved off past the van and out into the dark night. Hondo dragged each of the sacks back to the rear and tossed them into the van again.

He came back to the cab at once, climbed in, and slowly drove the van out into the arena. It moved very slowly across the basketball court and stopped directly under the far basket.

Through the whole vast arena, nothing moved now.

Every eye in the silent locker room was focused on the TV monitor. They all watched the police van drive out onto the floor, move slowly across, and come to a stop under the basket. The Owl players were breathing hard. The terrorists watched with bright, greedy eyes.

McVea spoke half to himself, fervently. "Okay, now the money. Come on!"

On the flickering monitor screen, Hondo appeared from the van cab, walked to the rear, opened the doors, and dragged out the two heavy sacks. He pulled the sacks out into the open court, and stopped.

"Jackpot!" McVea breathed in the locker room.

Alone in the enormous emptiness of the arena floor, Hondo left the sacks and walked deliberately to the deserted scorer's table. He picked up the public address microphone, then turned and looked straight into a closed-circuit TV camera.

"Your money's here, and your getaway van. Two million dollars in hundred-dollar bills. All used bills

126

and not in any serial-number order. The jet's waiting out at the airport. We've kept . . ."

In the locker room, the four terrorists smiled as they watched the monitor and Hondo looking straight at them.

". . . our bargain, exactly the way you wanted it. Now you start moving up here right now or the deal's off, and then you can just *whistle* for your money! Right now, you understand, or a *whistle* is all you get."

Ollie Wyatt sat by himself a few feet from where Don Benson lay on the locker-room floor. Ollie had been watching the TV monitor as closely as the others, but had looked away for a moment to the sweat-beaded face of his wounded friend. Now he suddenly looked back, stared at the screen. Hondo's voice was clear in the locker room. Ollie blinked at the screen, heard the faint, but clear emphasis Hondo's voice had put on the word whistle. Twice! Repeating the word, each time with the same slight emphasis. Ollie glanced quickly around. No one else seemed to have noticed it; the eyes of the four terrorists were all glued to the screen, watching the sacks of money out on the basketball court.

McVea turned to the players. "Wyatt! Morgan! And you three—" he pointed to three others,—"you're going to go up with us."

"What about the rest of 'em?" Rameri said.

"They stay down here," McVea said. "We don't need them."

Rameri shook his head. "We can't leave them behind us! We'll have enough to watch—"

"Leave 'em," Forrester said. "We made the deal."

"That's what I say too," Burke agreed.

McVea said, "We don't have the money, Rameri. Kill these players and we'll never get it."

127

Rameri looked around, but he said nothing. McVea nodded.

"Okay, you five, get moving!"

On the vast floor, Hondo spoke into the walkie-talkie hooked to his flak jacket. "Deke, you still in position?"

From the dark ventilating duct, Deke's voice came low. "In position."

"What's going on down there?"

"It looks like they're getting ready to move up. They're taking five of the players with them, including Ollie and Coach Morgan. They're leaving the rest."

"When they leave, get in there and help Benson, and then tail them up and hold position at the head of the ramp—out of sight."

"Check," Deke said softly. "Here they go! They're on the way!"

In the locker room, McVea pushed Ollie in front of him out the door into the corridor. His sharp eyes searched up and down, saw nothing.

"Okay, up the ramp, Wyatt—and very slow," McVea said.

Rameri came next with Coach Morgan. Burke covered one of the other players, and Forrester brought up the rear behind the last two hostages.

They moved up the ramp in a tense, silent file.

Hondo flicked the switches on his walkie-talkie. "We've got fifteen seconds while they're out of range of a TV monitor. Street and Luca hold position, don't give them a glimmer that you're there."

"Okay, Lieutenant," Street said from the loading entrance.

"I ain't even breathing," Luca said under the van.

Hondo went on, "T. J., swing down from those rafters while they can't spot you and take up a position inside the scoreboard where you can cover the whole basketball floor."

He watched for a moment as T. J. appeared in the rafters, dropped his rope, and rappelled down to the four-sided scoreboard that hung directly over the center of the basketball court. T. J. vanished inside the scoreboard, and the high rafters were deserted once more.

Hondo spoke again. "Deke, move in as soon as they're out of sight."

In the ventilating duct, Deke waited another sixty seconds. Then he pushed out the grille and dropped lightly down to the locker-room floor.

"Hey!" an Owl player cried.

The others jumped to their feet, their eyes on Deke's rifle.

"It's okay, Police S.W.A.T.," Deke said. "Just stay right where you all are."

"Boy!" big Sandy Agee said, "I never thought I'd be so glad to see the fuzz!"

"Keep it quiet! They've still got your buddies," Deke said sharply. He hurried to where Bill Grainger was bending over Don Benson. "Let's look!"

Deke examined Benson quickly but efficiently. "Okay. He's bad, but I think he'll make it. Just keep him as quiet as you've been doing. We'll get a doctor down as fast as we can."

Deke stood up. "Everyone stay right here—and lock that door after me!"

He hurried out and moved silently up the ramp toward the arena floor above.

On the empty floor, Hondo left the scorer's desk and walked to the sacks of money lying near the van.

For a long minute, he stood there alone.

Then McVea appeared at the top of the ramp up from the locker room, Ollie Wyatt walking slowly in front of him. McVea's automatic rifle was touching Ollie's back.

McVea paused at the top of the ramp, looked slowly all around. Then he walked forward cautiously.

Behind him Rameri appeared, prodding Coach Morgan ahead of him. Then Burke came out with the third Owl player, his face glistening with sweat, licking nervously at his lips. The last two Owls, and Forrester, brought up the rear.

The whole group moved warily toward the spot where Hondo waited beside the sacks of money.

Halfway out, McVea motioned for everyone to stop. His cold eyes scanned the entire empty arena again, looked up and swept every beam and rafter, the front of the whole second deck, the empty windows of the broadcasting booth. He did it again, and stopped to look straight at something only once—at Robin Phillips standing alone in an aisle in the box seats. McVea smiled, made a small, mock bow of his head toward Robin. Then he turned to face Hondo and moved the whole group to a few feet from the S.W.A.T. leader. He looked Hondo up and down.

"So you're the chief fuzz?"

Hondo said, "And you're the patriot Arab leader."

For a long moment the two men stared at each other, neither dropping his gaze.

"Okay," McVea said. "I think we've got some business to do."

21

Hondo pointed. "Not until you release all the hostages."

McVea shook his head. "You know we have to keep some of them at least as far as the airport. You'll find the rest in the locker room. Unfortunately, a couple got too brave for their own good. One's dead, I'm afraid, but if you move this fast, you can save the other."

"Five is too many. Keep two, no more," Hondo said.

"Don't tell me! We keep the five."

"To the airport?" Hondo said. "And how far past that? All the way to your destination?"

"You'll find out," McVea said. "Look, just keep following orders the way you have, and no more of this high-priced help will get hurt. You got that?"

"I've got it," Hondo said.

"Good. Now open up those sacks and let's make sure what you've got inside."

In the group behind McVea, Rameri raised his rifle against Coach Pete Morgan's head. The coach stood rigid.

"Make sure all you bring out of those sacks is money," Rameri said.

Forrester raised his rifle. "Make real sure," he said.

"Yeh," Burke said, suddenly tougher again, the end in sight.

Hondo opened one sack, lifted it, and dumped packets of hundred dollar bills out onto the basketball floor. The small packets bounced and rolled in a green cascade. The four gunmen stared at the mound of money.

"Just like you said," Burke said to McVea. "The jackpot!"

"Look at all the beautiful green," Forrester breathed.

Rameri said, "We ain't out of here yet. Don't start spending it until we are."

"When are you going to believe it's worked, eh?" McVea said.

"When I'm counting it into a bank a long way from here," Rameri said. "Let's get moving, bright boy."

McVea nodded and said to Hondo, "Okay, put it all back in the sack, Lieutenant, and see that none happens to stick to your fingers. We don't give out tips."

Hondo gathered up the packets, stuffed them all back into the sack. McVea motioned with his rifle.

"Now the other sack. Not that I don't trust my fellow man, but moral standards are so low these days."

Hondo opened the second sack and dumped some of the money out, looking at McVea with contempt. McVea shrugged and took one more long, careful look around. Rameri had never stopped searching the stands, aisles and rafters for any sign of an ambush. McVea seemed satisfied. He faced Hondo again.

"Now throw your gun aside," he commanded.

Hondo hesitated.

"Do it!" Rameri shouted. "And fast! Or one of these hotshot athletes goes right now!"

Hondo hesitated for another moment. Then he tossed his carbine aside. It clattered across the hardwood floor, the noise echoing in the cavernous arena. McVea and Rameri watched it but made no move to pick it up.

"Check inside the van," McVea said to Forrester.

132

Rameri said, "I'll check the van. Watch the great coach."

He held his automatic rifle in front of him and moved carefully forward toward Hondo, who stood between him and the van. Hondo didn't move, never took his eyes off Rameri. Rameri stopped a few feet away and motioned with the rifle.

"Move away from the van. Now!"

His eyes fixed on Rameri, Hondo moved aside, backing up to a spot some twenty feet away. No one noticed that his movement took him almost halfway to where his carbine lay; all eyes were focused on the sacks of money and the van that would take them to safety.

"That's far enough," Rameri said.

He moved the rest of the way to the van. He approached it lightly, moving on the balls of his feet like a boxer half his size. He reached out with his rifle and swung the rear doors open one at a time, moving behind each door as it swung open, missing nothing. His gun ready, he moved up close and peered all around inside.

Then he walked to the front of the van and opened the cab doors just as carefully. He stood looking at the empty cab; then he turned and nodded to McVea.

"It's all clear in the van," Rameri said, his husky voice implying that if he said so you could count on it.

He looked up and completely scanned the stands and rafters once more.

"All clean as a baby's tail," he announced with finality. He turned toward McVea and the others still in a knot some twenty feet from the money and the van. "Let's get out of here."

McVea motioned quickly, and Burke and Forrester prodded Ollie and the others forward. They all approached the van and the bags of money in a close-

133

knit group, Ollie and the other Owls in front, McVea and his gunmen shielded by them and holding their rifles hard against their backs.

At the rear of the van McVea stopped them, glanced once toward Hondo still standing aside where Rameri had sent him, and prodded Ollie.

"Okay, Wyatt, you and those three pick up the sacks and toss them inside the van."

Ollie and the three players picked up the money, two men to each sack, and tossed them into the back of the van. Coach Morgan watched them, looking around helplessly. McVea waved them away, looked into the van for a final check, stepped back, and smiled toward Hondo.

"I guess that's bingo. Thanks for everything, Lieutenant. We'll see you, or the other fuzz, at the airport. Just keep on playing it nice and cool and everyone's okay." He laughed at Hondo's grim face and looked at Ollie. "Okay, everyone inside. You first, Wyatt."

Ollie climbed up and into the back of the van, leaving both doors open.

Hondo glanced once toward his carbine, thrust his fingers into his mouth, and whistled shrilly twice.

The whistles echoed and reverberated through the vast, hollow arena.

Exactly the way they had when Ollie Wyatt had whistled the old high-school-play signal in the S.W.A.T. command room!

McVea whirled toward Hondo.

Rameri raised his rifle in alarm where he stood at the front of the van.

Burke and Forrester swung left, right, all around.

Ollie dove back out through the open rear van doors, and rolled hard into Coach Morgan and the other three Owl players. They all went down in a sprawling heap while the four terrorists turned in every direction searching for the danger, the reason for Hondo's whistled signal.

For a long moment the five Owls were out of the action, out of the direct line of fire.

Hondo dove for his carbine, grabbed it in a long roll, and came up on his feet firing.

High in the scoreboard, T. J. opened fire with his deadly sniper's rifle. He fired twice, and Burke and Forrester were both hit, flung to the floor by the force of the high-powered weapon. They lay without moving, their arms flung out, their rifles clattering across the hardwood floor.

McVea, grazed by one of Hondo's shots, fell on his side, still holding his rifle.

Hondo swung toward Rameri at the front of the van. Rameri didn't wait—he dove for the cover of the van's front wheels. Hondo dropped flat to get a better shot.

"Lieutenant!" It was McVea's voice.

Hondo looked up. McVea stood holding Ollie Wyatt, his rifle under Ollie's chin. He prodded viciously. Ollie's head jerked backwards.

"I ought to kill him right now!" McVea said savagely, breathing hard and holding his left arm tight against his side to stop the bleeding from his grazed shoulder. "All right, no more games. You made your play, congratulations, but it fell short. Now we get out of here!"

Rameri came out from under the front of the van and walked toward McVea, his snakelike eyes fixed on Hondo, who stood alone with his carbine on the wide floor.

"Nice try, big fuzz, but no cigar," Rameri said.

"Not another shot, or Wyatt gets it right now,"

135

McVea said. "Throw that damned gun away again! Do it!"

"To hell with that," Rameri snarled. "I'm gonna kill me this one right now!"

Rameri raised his rifle.

22

McVea knocked Rameri's rifle up. "No! We'll take the wise-guy fuzz with us! Superstar and supercop! *All* the way!"

Rameri swore, for a split second turned his rifle toward McVea. "I told you not to do that—"

"Idiot! We need two good host—" McVea began.

In that instant, with the two gunmen facing each other and Ollie Wyatt forgotten for the moment, Dom Luca came out from under the van with his shotgun blasting.

Rameri's rifle was exploded out of his hands.

McVea went down flat, struggling to get his rifle turned toward Luca.

Luca dove at Ollie, taking the basketball star down to the floor, firing his shotgun again with one hand. The load went high. McVea stood.

"The van!" he shouted.

Weaponless, Rameri didn't need any urging. As Luca struggled to get a good aim, the two gunmen reached the van cab, jumped in, and started it up. Behind the wheel, McVea slammed the vehicle into gear and roared off across the floor toward the far end of the court. The wall loomed like an express train rushing at the van.

McVea jammed on the brakes, slewed the van in a wide skidding turn away from the wall, hurtled back toward the center of the court. Dom Luca's shotgun blast went wide again, taking a chunk of sheet metal off the van roof. The van bore down on Luca and Ollie Wyatt.

The two men ran.

Still the van bore down on them, McVea's eyes savage behind the wheel, Rameri trying to get a shot with McVea's rifle.

Luca and Ollie dove over the first row of seats and the van swung in a long, screaming skid going away.

"The locker room," McVea said through clenched teeth.

Rameri nodded.

The van raced across the floor.

Deke Kay appeared on the locker-room ramp, dropped onto his belly in the narrow space, and fired straight at the oncoming van.

The bullets slammed through the windshield, and McVea swung the van screaming again, heading for the entrance at the loading ramp.

Jim Street appeared, down on one knee, firing his automatic rifle.

"They're everywhere! Damn, damn!" McVea shouted. He turned the van once more and roared back into the arena.

"Damn you!" Rameri cried, "keep going out the loading entrance! Run that bastard over! Get us out of here!"

"He's got too clear a shot at us coming at him!" McVea shouted. "There's got to be a way at the other end!"

137

"They've got us boxed in, you big brain!" Rameri raged. "And the money's in the van!"

Ahead of them, T. J. came sliding down his rope from the scoreboard and joined Hondo kneeling beside the fallen Burke and Forrester. Both S.W.A.T. men aimed at the onrushing van. McVea turned once more.

"The loading entrance!" Rameri raged. "It's the only way! Just one of them!"

McVea nodded and gunned the van toward the open door at the far end of the court. Jim Street still knelt in the wide entrance. He saw the truck coming. He looked quickly behind him, then to his right, and got up and ran toward the side of the open ramp. He yanked a lever and dove out of the line of fire into the stands.

Rameri poured fire at the point where Street had vanished. He leaned out the cab window and fired behind him at Hondo, T. J., Luca, and Deke, who were all converging in pursuit.

"Jesus!" McVea shouted. He pointed ahead.

Activated by Street, who had pulled the lever, the heavy steel door was coming down across the wide freight entrance.

Instinctively McVea started to brake.

"Keep going!" Rameri snarled.

"We'll never make it!" McVea cried.

Rameri pointed his rifle at McVea.

"I said keep going!" Rameri said.

"It's suicide!"

"You want to live forever?"

"No, we'll hit head on! We'll—"

"Yes!" Rameri said. "For you, it's suicide if you don't make it out!"

He cocked the automatic rifle, held it to McVea's

head. McVea looked once at Rameri, then jammed down the accelerator.

The van raced toward the rapidly closing steel freight door. McVea licked his dry lips, staring only ahead. Rameri watched the door coming down. Both men sat rigid, transfixed, their eyes hypnotized by the slowly lowering door and the dark, open night outside—the night that meant freedom if they could just make it through.

They were less than fifty feet from freedom.

The S.W.A.T. team was firing at them now from behind and both sides. They didn't even see the bullets or hear them.

The door was past the halfway point—there was no more room for the hurtling van.

McVea jammed down the brake.

The van screamed in a long skid, slammed sideways into the now closed steel gate, bounced back, and came to a shuddering halt crosswise on the loading entrance ramp.

Rameri recovered from the impact, kicked out the broken door on his side, and leaped out. McVea dove after him, both men hitting the concrete behind the van.

The S.W.A.T. team ran toward them on the far side of the shattered van.

"Die, you bastards!" Rameri screamed out. Behind the cover of the van, he laid his automatic rifle on the steaming hood and opened fire.

The S.W.A.T. team hit the hard floor, returning the fire in a heavy fusillade.

Rameri fired back, unable to fire low enough, but for the moment pinning the S.W.A.T. team down.

"We're finished, bright boy!" Rameri raged, firing out into the arena. "You blew it!"

"We'll deal!" McVea cried. "We'll cop a plea! Stop firing, you idiot!"

"Twenty years? Maybe life? You cop a plea, bright boy! I'm not going inside for the rest of my life!" Rameri yelled.

"There's always an angle, you fool! A good shyster, a bleeding heart jury! But if you kill a cop, kill anyone else, they'll throw the book at—"

Rameri looked back at McVea. "An angle, bright boy? A scheme? Another big plan? You and your big brain, the smart hotshot! Yeh, and what do we get —nothing! What do we pay a shyster with? Nothing!"

"Rameri—" McVea began.

"You blew it, bright boy," Rameri said, his hoarse voice icy now. "You let a two-bit lieutenant ambush us! Okay, it's over! I told you we'd find out when it was over! Let's see what you've got in those technicolor guts of yours! Let's see what color you are inside, bright boy!"

He turned his rifle on McVea. McVea jumped toward him. For a long moment the two faced each other behind the cover of the van, all firing stopped now, the great arena echoing only to silence.

"You stupid ape!" McVea said.

"Gutless bright boy!" Rameri snarled.

Rameri's finger squeezed the trigger. He grinned his shark grin. The automatic rifle exploded in a ragged volley.

A volley that went high and wide.

As Rameri fell backwards on the concrete, the long, thin knife was sticking up out of his ribs.

McVea looked down at the dead man. He curled his lips in a faint sneer, spat deliberately on the dead Rameri's face.

Then he stepped out around the shattered van, his hands high above his head.

"Don't shoot! I'm alone! I surrender!"

He walked slowly toward the S.W.A.T. team. All through the great arena patrolmen were running forward. Robin Phillips ran toward Ollie, Coach Morgan, and the three other Owl players, all of whom were smiling and slapping each other's backs as if they'd just won the big game. In a way they had—the biggest game.

Hondo and the S.W.A.T. team reached McVea.

"Cuff him!" Hondo said. "Deke, get some ambulances, and get a doctor down to Benson fast. Street, check out all the Owl players, see if they need any help, take their statements, get them food and something to drink. T. J., go get Joanane Wyatt and take her to Ollie."

Luca and Deke turned McVea around roughly, cuffed him, and turned him back to face Hondo. Luca remained to one side, his shotgun trained on McVea while the others went off on their errands. McVea's shoulder was still bleeding, but his shoulder wasn't what was on his mind.

"He's back there," McVea said, nodding his head toward the battered van. "He was insane. Joseph Rameri, a crazy man! It was his scheme, he made the plan. I guess we were crazy to even listen to him. After a while we wanted to stop, but he made us go on. He killed that Solly Beckberg, shot Benson. In the end, I had to stop him myself."

"Hey," Luca said, "I think this dum-dum wants us to give him a medal!"

"He just went crazy," McVea said. "We were all afraid of him. Ask the others if they're alive."

"One is, one isn't," Hondo said. "Bad luck for you. The young one's alive, and he's already told us his story."

McVea nodded slowly. "Okay, only it was Rameri who did all the killing. I didn't want that. I just wanted the money."

"Yeh," Hondo said. "You want to tell me your name now?"

"Why not? It's McVea—Douglas McVea."

Hondo smiled thinly. "That sure is an odd name for an Arab terrorist."

They stood looking at each other for a moment. Then McVea shrugged.

"It was worth a try, wasn't it?"

"Just barely," Hondo said, and he nodded to Luca. "Take him to the van."

In the S.W.A.T. war room the next morning, with McVea and Burke in the city jail's medical ward, Hondo, Deke, Jim Street, and Luca groaned over the reports they had to write for headquarters. Chief Roman and Warren Royce had been in to congratulate the team. The chief was happy as a clam over the success of the S.W.A.T. idea.

"He could at least have had someone else do the reports for heros like us," Luca said.

The door opened, and T. J. came in with Ollie and Joanne Wyatt. Ollie was carrying a basketball. He held it out to Hondo.

"Here you go, Lieutenant," Ollie said. "Every guy on the team signed it. Don Benson too. He's going to be okay."

Hondo held the basketball, looked at it in delight.

"I'm not even going to say you didn't have to," Hondo said. "Thanks."

"Just a small token from a lot of guys who're lucky you and the S.W.A.T. team were around," Ollie said.

Joanne added, "And not nearly enough to say how grateful we all are."

"What my foxy old lady is saying is, how do you say thanks for saving someone's life?" Ollie said.

Luca said, "Hey, how about some free tickets!"

"You got 'em," Ollie said.

"No, he hasn't," Hondo said. "That's against department rules, sorry."

Luca threw up his hands. "Everything I want is too expensive, or against department rules!"

They all laughed. Hondo nodded seriously to Ollie. "Good thing you remembered your old 'whistle' play."

"Remember it? Coach is putting it in our playbook," Ollie said.

Joanne said, "Is it against department rules for us to invite everybody to our place for dinner tonight? Real, homemade soul food!"

"Hondo," Deke said, "if you say it's against the rules, you're going to have a bunch of *real* revolutionaries on your hands."

Hondo grinned. "We accept, with thanks—as long as it isn't pizza!"

"Now, Lieutenant," Joanne said. "You ever hear of soul-food pizza?"

Everyone laughed again—except Dom Luca.

"What's so funny?" Luca said, straight-faced. "My mom's been making that for years."

Jim Street threw a book at him. The reports forgotten for the moment, they began to talk about the plans for dinner tonight, who would bring what, and about the way the Owls were going to sweep right through the playoffs now.

Hondo sat and watched them. But he wasn't thinking of soul food or basketball. He was thinking of Captain Dawson, down and dying on that long-ago slum street with the seven other victims of the bloody crossfire that day.

"We got to . . . learn . . . how to . . . do this," the dying Dawson said thickly. *"No one . . . should . . . get . . . hurt . . . except them!"*

Silently Hondo apologized once again to Dawson. Back then he hadn't known what it was like. Now he knew, and knew that Dawson had done his best. A brave man, Dawson, and maybe he'd be pleased

143

now, wherever he was. The job had been done here. No one had been hurt except the criminals, and S.W.A.T. had proven what it could do.

Hondo smiled. The job had been done, and done right.